ACCLAIM FOR JANICE THOMPSON'S BELLA STORIES

"Bella Rossi is one of my all-time favorite characters in a contemporary romantic comedy, and Janice Thompson is at the top of my list when it comes to must read fiction! When I found out she was writing a series of stories called The Bella Novella Collection, I had them on my wish list before you could say Dean Martin!"
—DEENA PETERSON, READER

"I'm pretty sure Bella is my favorite book character of all time, and I was more than excited to find out Janice Thompson has brought us back into her life. In this first installment in the novella series, Bella is back to doing what she does best - pulling off impossibly perfect wedding ceremonies. We also get to connect with DJ and the rest of Bella's crazy family. I was excited to see Hannah, Gabi, and Scarlett also included in this series, and know their stories get to continue for us."
—KAREN, READER

"Bella never fails to capture the reader's attention and pull you in to the chaos of the Rossi family all the while leading you to the One who makes order out of our chaos. Can't wait to read the next installment."
—MCKINSEY JONES, READER

"Bella and the Rossi clan are back and I couldn't be happier! Bella is, once again, planning a fabulous wedding to top all weddings. It is to be held the week before Christmas under the stars.....nothing could go wrong........right? When things don't go as planned (but then this isn't surprising when planning an outdoor wedding in December....even if it is in Texas), Bella and all of the Rossi clan step up to the plate to make this wedding a celestial event no one will ever forget. I was so happy to read this book and felt like I was among old friends again....even the Splendora Sisters are back! This is a must read and if you haven't read the other Bella books by Janice Thompson, go grab them right now and get to reading them. They are ALL wonderful. Janice is one of my very favorite authors because I love Christian fiction and she knows how to write it."

—AMAZON READER

"Mama Mia, let's escape! Let's fall in love! Let's eat Chicken Parmesan, Fettuccine Alfredo, and Bubba's down-home barbecue without gaining a pound. It's all possible when we hang out with Bella Rossi! You'll root for the Rossi and Neeley families as they break down cultural barriers and rush toward each other, arms wide open."

—TRISH PERRY, AUTHOR, *BEACH DREAMS* AND *THE GUY I'M NOT DATING*

The Bella Novella Collection
Book One

Once Upon
a Moonlight
Night

JANICE THOMPSON

DEDICATION

To Maddy, my little nature lover.

Wherever you go, no matter what the weather, always bring your own sunshine.

—*Anthony J. D'Angelo*

Chapter One

BLUE SKIES

"I once dated a weather girl, we talked up a storm."
— Jay London

When a girl is raised in a wacky Italian family, certain things are a given. For instance, she can always count on drama around the dinner table. Someone's always trying to out-holler someone else, or get his—or her—point across. And when your family is in business together, the volume can get even louder.

That's why, when my Aunt Rosa interrupted our evening meal to announce that she and Uncle Laz were going on a three week vacation to Italy, the volume around the Rossi dinner table rose to a deafening roar. Really? Rosa and Laz, gone for three whole weeks...during the holidays? How would the family survive without them? More importantly, what would we eat at our Friday evening family dinners?

"Are you serious, Rosa?" Mama called out across the ruckus. She reached for a cloth napkin and used it to fan herself. "*Three* weeks?"

To my right, one of my twin daughters started to fuss in her highchair. I glanced over at ten-month-old Holly and gave her a bite of pasta. Out of the corner of my eye I caught a glimpse of Ivy, tossing bites of the soft pasta onto the floor. Not that anyone noticed. They were far too focused on my aunt and uncle.

"That's right." Aunt Rosa beamed, her eyes sparkling with delight. "Three glorious weeks in the Old Country, touring from one city to the next. Visiting my cousins and their children. Laz and I haven't been back home since our honeymoon a few years ago, and we can't wait to go back."

She lit into a lengthy explanation of the various places they planned to visit, but lost me when she mentioned Tuscany. Sounded heavenly, but with so much on my proverbial plate—four kids, a husband who ran his own construction business and my work at Club Wed—the idea of traveling seemed like an elusive dream, at best.

Still, from the shimmer in Uncle Laz's eyes, I could tell he was fully onboard for this idea. I'd never seen him look so happy. Or so tired. If anyone deserved a vacation, he and Rosa did.

My other family members seemed a little less enthusiastic. I understood why, of course. Losing Rosa and Laz for the better part of a month could potentially wreck us all. Or, at least our stomachs.

"B-but if you leave, who's going to cook for us?" Pop reached for one of Rosa's famous garlic twists from the platter in the center of the table and tore off a piece. "We'll all starve to death." He shoved the bread into his mouth and glared at my aunt.

"True, that." I did my best not to sigh aloud. After all, Rosa and Laz did most of the cooking in the Rossi household. For as long as I could remember, their talents in the kitchen had kept us well fed and happy.

Mama paled. "I guess it's time I stepped up to the plate.

Rosa has been slaving away in our kitchen for years, poor thing. I suppose it's my turn." She reached for her napkin and fanned her face, then mumbled something about how she hoped we all survived her cooking.

"Slaving away?" The wrinkles around Rosa's eyes deepened and she grew misty. "Since when is cooking anything but pure delight?"

Judging from the look in Mama's eyes, she felt a bit panicked. No doubt this announcement had her reeling. She would be left alone to man—er, woman—the Rossi kitchen.

My brother Armando gazed with sadness at Uncle Laz. "It will be the end of the Rossi family as we know it, wait and see. You will come back from Italy to find that we've wasted away to nothing. I'll be skin and bones."

Hardly. The boy could drop twenty pounds and still have plenty of padding, especially around the mid-section. Of course, I would never say that.

"Don't be so dramatic." His wife Scarlet slapped his hand. "I'll keep you well fed." She giggled and her cheeks flamed pink.

"I know you will, baby." He reached over to give her a tender kiss. "At least I know we'll always have dessert." He quirked a brow and I realized he wasn't just talking about food anymore. Ick. These two were definitely still honeymooners at heart.

"Look on the bright side, everyone," Mama said. "If you don't like my cooking, you can always eat at Parma John's."

"Yes, that's right." Nick, my oldest brother, added his thoughts from across the table. "I'll be serving up pizzas, pasta and salads at the restaurant every day, as usual. So, Rosa and Laz aren't the only ones in the family who can keep you well fed." My brother squared his shoulders, the Rossi pride shining through on his face.

"And if you ever want something sweet, you can always come to my bakery," Scarlet added.

I breathed a visible sigh of relief. Nick and Scarlet had a point. We ate a good portion of our meals at Parma John's anyway, especially on the days when Nick served the Mambo Italiano Special—a yummy Dean Martin themed pizza pie. Suddenly I felt much better about Rosa and Laz's decision to travel. We would survive without them.

"If anyone deserves a great vacation, it's you two." I gave my Aunt what I hoped would look like a convincing smile. "I've never known two people who worked harder than you and Laz. You cook for us, help out at Parma John's, and star in your own television show on The Food Network. And you help with every wedding, to boot. Who else could handle so much and still stay sane?"

"No one ever accused me of being sane." Uncle Laz gave me a little wink. "But I'm tired just listening to the list of all we do. You've just confirmed it for me, Bella. It's time for a break."

"Thanks a lot, Bella." Armando sighed. "Convince them to go. Great idea. We're all so grateful."

"I think they deserve a vacation," I said. "We all do."

"I'm not questioning your decision to go." Pop scooped up a mound of pasta onto his fork. "Just the timing. It's almost Thanksgiving. Who's going to make the turkey and dressing? And the pies?"

Deafening silence filled the room as we all turned to face them. Without Rosa's familiar dishes, the holiday would seem strangely off-kilter.

Rosa dabbed her lips with her napkin then reached for her water glass. "Oh, don't worry about that. We're not leaving until the Saturday after Thanksgiving. We fly out on the 28th. So, expect the usual feast on Thanksgiving day." She took a sip from her glass and put it back down.

A visible sigh of relief sounded from all in attendance, and the clinking of silverware kicked in again as folks dove back into their food. I breathed in the luscious aroma of the manicotti's sauce. The yummy scent hovered in the air around us. No matter how many years I'd lived in my own house with D.J., I still loved these twice-weekly dinners with my family in my childhood home.

Ah…D.J. How I loved that man of mine. Of course, I loved everyone seated around the table. What's not to love in an Italian family, after all?

My family hailed from Italy, by way of New Jersey. How we landed on Galveston Island was a story that led back to my Aunt Bianca, Uncle Laz's first wife. Quite the tale.

We Rossi's pretty much melted in the heat those first few years in Texas, but slowly acclimated to both the extreme humidity and the hot summers. We wouldn't go back to New Jersey now, even if the governor issued a personal invitation. Still, our version of "Texan" varied a bit from the norm. Yes, a few of us wore cowboy boots on occasion. And true, we'd learned to say y'all. Several of us had even learned the Texas two-step. But no one—stress, no one—in the Rossi clan could hold a candle to D.J. when it came to being an authentic Texan. That boy ate, slept and breathed cowboy. Hunky. Delicious. All-American with apple pie on top cowboy. And I'd fallen head over heels for him the moment I'd clamped eyes on him the first time. The boy knocked me off my feet. Literally. Our first evening together I'd hit the floor. Passed out cold. Okay, so that incident had a little something to do with stress over a misunderstanding related to my new job as

5

coordinator at Club Wed, but still. . .his cowboyish ways had bowled me over.

And now, years later, he was mine. . .all mine. Well, mine. . .and my family's. We Rossis knew how to sweep people in, and no better place than the dining room table.

Surrounding myself with family was amazing, of course, but nothing could top the food. Not with Aunt Rosa and Uncle Laz creating the menus and preparing the meals.

I reached to fill my plate once again, sighing as I realized I'd already had too much. Still, who could blame me? Heaven help the poor soul trying to diet in our family. The temptations on a night like tonight would probably do them in. Who could resist, especially with my aunt and uncle at the helm. Their ethnic Italian fare, rich in flavor, captivated the imagination with their savory sauces and robust spices. Not to mention the fact that Aunt Rosa grew her own tomatoes—Romas—in the backyard, along with basil, rosemary, cilantro and much more. Having access to the finest vegetables made all the difference, and it showed in every meal the duo cooked—whether they were preparing dishes for the family or cooking in front of television audiences for their Food Network Show, *The Italian Kitchen*. Authentic Mediterranean cuisine at its finest—rich, tasty, and hearty—and all mine for the taking as I gathered together with family on a night like tonight. Just what a girl needed after a long day's work. A true celebration of life, love and family.

I took another bite of the manicotti, enjoying its hearty flavor, rich with spices. The gooey mozzarella oozed from the shells, dribbling down onto my plate below. I managed to catch it with my tongue, but got sauce on my chin in the process. My sweet hubby reached over with his napkin and dabbed it off, then gave me a little kiss on the cheek. I winked at him, and the butterfly farm in my stomach set to flight, just as it had done that very first day I'd met him.

"No PDA at the table," Pop called out.

I knew what he meant, of course: Public displays of affection.

"Hey, we're old married people now," I countered. "Remember?"

"I would hope so, what with the four kids and all." My father let out a raucous laugh then ripped a garlic roll in half and stuck a piece in his mouth.

Oh, the feelings of joy that swept over me in that moment. So much could be said about the experience of eating with my family, but only one word came to mind at the moment: homey. I always felt bonded—with the people, the food, the whole experience. Other families experienced this feeling at Thanksgiving and Christmas, perhaps, but we Rossis didn't wait for the holidays. We ate together as often—and as much—as possible. And no one—stress, no one—got up from the table until they were full. Very, very full.

Still, as I caught a glimpse of Mama, I had to admit, she still looked a bit worried. "How long will you and Laz stay in Europe?" she asked Aunt Rosa. "Will you be gone during the Christmas holidays?"

"We arrive home on the 18th of December, in plenty of time to prepare for Christmas." Rosa clasped her hands together at her ample chest. "But we want to see all of the sights in Europe that we can. We're starting in Italy of course, and will go from there."

"Oh, and Paris. Don't forget Paris." Laz stabbed the manicotti with his fork, then dropped it onto his plate.

"But, what about your show?" my mother asked. "Do the people at The Food Network know you're going to be gone for so long?"

"That's the best part." Rosa reached across the table and snagged the butter. "We're not filming for the entire month of December, so the timing couldn't be better."

Maybe. Or maybe not. Concern overtook me as I thought of one complication. "But Rosa, what about the Collins' wedding?"

From the moment I'd taken over management of Club Wed, our family's premiere wedding facility at the old Victorian home next door to my parents' house, Rosa and Laz had participated in every event, catering, baking, serving and wowing guests with their culinary skills. How could I manage without them, especially with such a busy season ahead? Ack.

Crinkles formed around Rosa's tired eyes. "Which wedding is that, again, Bella?" she asked. "I don't recognize the name."

"Justine Collins. Remember? The meteorologist from Channel Eleven? She's marrying the scientist guy? The one with the PBS show for kids? The guy who likes stars? You were going to make the star-shaped pasta for their wedding on the 19th of December."

"Wait. A man who likes stars?" Pop wrinkled his nose as he loaded his fork with pasta. "What kind of a man likes stars? Is this one of those Hollywood-types? Some friend of Brock Benson's?" The mound of linguini disappeared into his mouth in one bite.

"Not movie stars, Cosmo." Mama rolled her eyes. "The kind in the sky. He studies them or some such thing."

Pop swallowed and took a swig of water. "Still sounds like a weird job for a man, if you ask me."

"Harold is very famous," I explained. "He's got his own show on PBS. It's an astronomy show for kids. And we've been working on this celestial themed wedding for months now. They're getting married on December 19th because— supposedly—there's a full moon and the stars are going to put on a show. Oh, and the weather is supposed to be absolutely ideal that day, according to Justine."

"Put on a show?" Armando looked perplexed by this idea.

"From what I can gather, they're going to be more visible and appear in greater number than before. Not that I'm one to stargaze. I'm usually too busy to look up." I took a sip of water and tried to still my heart. "My point is, the sky is going to be pretty amazing that night. This, according to the meteorologist bride."

She's got pretty clear vision to see all the way from now until then," Pop said.

"Sounds like we're going to be even busier than ever with this wedding." Mama sighed. "With Rosa gone, we'll be at a loss."

We all turned once again to look at Rosa and Laz, who didn't seem the least bit concerned, judging from the mouthfuls of food they continued to consume.

"Now don't fret!" Rosa paused to take a drink. "We're coming home on the 18th, as I said, so I will be here just in time to help with the wedding. No worries!"

Relief flooded over me. "Really? Oh, that's perfect."

"I plan to sleep for days after I get home." Laz stretched and his extended belly and patted it with his palms, making a drum sound. "So don't wake me to help with this wedding."

Rosa gave him a knowing look and he sighed. "Okay, okay. Wake me up. But don't expect me to help. Much."

"But you promised to make the sauce—er, *gravy*—Laz," I said. "No one can do it like you."

"True." My uncle pushed his chair back and stood—slowly, his arthritis making the move difficult—and then leaned down to kiss Rosa on the cheek. Everyone at the table stopped eating long enough to watch the two of them. . .and sigh. Just a few years back, Rosa and Laz couldn't stand each another. Now they were happily married and headed back to Italy for a second honeymoon. Who were we to stop them?

Out of the corner of my eye, I caught a glimpse of my father, who was strangely silent. No doubt he struggled with the idea of Rosa and Laz leaving, and not just because of the food. My parents shared a home with my aunt and uncle, after all. They did everything together. With Rosa and Laz away, nothing would be the same for my Mama and Pop.

I shifted my gaze to my hubby. D.J. seemed oblivious as he took a bite of the steaming manicotti. Oh well. At least we wouldn't go hungry at the Neeley house. I'd acquired a few of Rosa's cooking skills, after all. Not that I had much time to spend in the kitchen, not with the big Collins wedding coming up. Still, I wouldn't waste time fretting over the future. I wasn't a weather forecaster like Justine. I couldn't see into tomorrow. Clear skies or cloudy, I couldn't predict. So, instead, I would simply settle in and enjoy the blue skies that hovered over me at this very moment as I ate the food I loved, surrounded by the people I adored. Really, could life get any finer?

Chapter Two

IT'S A LOVELY DAY TOMORROW

"On cable TV they have a weather channel—24 hours of weather. We had something like that where I grew up. We called it a window." — Dan Spencer

After hearing about Rosa and Laz's travel plans, I could hardly focus on my work. I couldn't put my finger on why the news bothered me so much, but it did. In spite of my passionate "They deserve a vacation" speech, having the family separated felt. . .wrong. Still, the show must go on, and all that, so I did what came naturally—buried myself in wedding preparations.

The next couple of days were spent wrapping up the plan for the Collins wedding, just one month away. What a glorious day that would be. I could hardly wait!

Wednesday—hump day—rolled around and I braced myself for the incoming cyclone that was Justine. Though tiny—the girl barely tipped the scale at a hundred pounds on her five-foot frame, I would guess—the blonde pixie whirled like a mini-tornado. This vivacious personality was suited for television, no doubt, but tended to wear me out.

Still, I adored her, hyper or not. And by the time she arrived for our previously scheduled meeting at Club Wed, I had all of my proverbial ducks in a row. Er, stars in alignment. I felt secure in the fact that I could pull off this celestial extravaganza, even without my aunt and uncle around to help with the finer points.

Justine arrived at the wedding facility looking like something out of a fashion magazine. The little diva was always dressed to kill, and today was no different. I'd never seen an ensemble like the one she wore. The blouse was white eyelet but the skirt—wow—was covered in tiny umbrellas. Not cheesy, but clever. Artistic. Cool.

"Love the skirt," I said, and then gave an admiring whistle. "Cool beans."

"Oh, my grandmother made it. Can you tell it's homemade? Most of my clothes are."

"No way." I gestured for her to turn around and she did. "It looks like something Gabi would dream up."

"Gabi Delgado's amazing, by the way. Thank you for recommending her to make my wedding dress. Best decision ever." Justine's expression grew dreamy, in a Disney Princess-y sort of way. "The gown she's designed is covered in Austrian crystals that sparkle like the stars in the sky. I've honestly never seen anything like the things she comes up with. Exquisite. Way too pretty for a magazine, even. You know?"

"Yep. And I'm always happy to recommend her. I'm happy to recommend all of my vendors. They made the cut because they're amazing." Still, something puzzled me about this conversation. "Justine, if your grandmother can sew, why isn't she making your wedding dress?"

The bride-to-be's eyes widened at this question. "Ooh, she was terrified when I suggested it. And I want her to be relaxed, to enjoy the experience of watching her only granddaughter get married. You know? My family's waited a long time to see me walk the aisle and I want them to love every minute. Can't imagine asking them to work my wedding." Justine laughed, but I didn't join in. I couldn't imagine *not* asking my family members to help with a wedding. Then again, we were in the wedding business.

I led the way to my office and gestured for Justine to have a seat. She chose to stand. The anxious bride paced my office, hands wringing and her eyes sparkling. "Bella, I can't tell you how excited we are about our big day. It's going to be perfect. Absolutely, totally perfect." She whipped out a stack of papers from her large handbag and plopped them on my desk. "We've come up with a final plan. I hope you're able to accommodate us, though I suspect it's going to be a challenge."

"O-oh?"

"Maybe. But I can promise you this, Bella. . .it's going to be the best wedding ever! People will be talking about it for years to come."

"I'm sure it will be amazing, since you came up with all of it." I took a seat in my chair and gestured once again for her to grab the empty chair opposite my desk. This starry-eyed gal had a lot to say and I'd better listen closely.

She sat and pointed to the paper on top. "I've written down everything. Every. Single. Detail. I've left nothing out."

"I can see that. Impressive."

Her finger traveled down the paper, landing on the word *celestial*. "So, naturally we're thinking stars. It will be a starry, starry night."

"Well, we can't really control that part, can we?" A nervous laugh wriggled up. "Hopefully it will be a starry night, as you've predicted, but one never knows."

13

"Oh, I'm sure it will be. Trust me, I've spent hours researching. But I'm talking about decorations. We need stars hanging in the gazebo."

"Gazebo? Wait. You're planning an outdoor ceremony? In December?" How could this little fact have escaped me? Surely I would've remembered an outdoor Christmas wedding.

Justine's nose wrinkled. "Well, of course. I can't imagine getting married indoors. In a stuffy room? With the open skies beckoning, the stars twinkling, the moon beaming, the heavens crying out for attention? What else did you think I meant when I said a celestial celebration?"

"Well, I, um. . ."

The bride-to-be's eyes sparkled as she clutched her hands together at her chest. "We chose the 19th of December not just because of the display of stars, but because the weather is supposed to be absolutely perfect that day. Unseasonably warm. In the mid-sixties. And yes, the skies are supposed to be clear and stars bright. Not a cloud in the sky, so we'll see every last one of them, twinkling away, just for us."

"You can really project that far ahead?" I asked.

"Project is the right word." A little grin tipped up the edges of her lips. "I hate to brag, but my weather predictions are usually spot-on. Remember yesterday when the meteorologist from Channel Two said it was going to rain all day?"

I didn't, but Justine didn't give me time to respond, anyway.

"He was wrong. I called it. Twenty percent chance, but hovering clouds lifted at noon and we had the most beautiful day ever."

Clouds weren't the only thing hovering right about now. Rosa hovered in the open doorway, dust cloth in hand.

Wrinkles formed around the edges of her lips as she stepped inside my office and started dusting the bookshelves. I looked her way. "Did you need me, Rosa?"

"Well. . ." She stopped dusting and glanced at Justine. "I don't mean to pry, but I overheard what you ladies were discussing. Not trying to be nosy, of course, but I think you should have a backup plan, just in case. You know? The outdoor wedding idea sounds wonderful, but what if your predictions are wrong?"

Justine's cheeks turned red. "Well, I never claimed to get it right *all* of the time, but hopefully things will swing my way this time."

"I hope so, honey." Rosa gave her a warm smile. "But even if the skies are cloudy, it'll be bright and sunny in your heart on your wedding day." She then lit into a lengthy story about the day she married Uncle Laz, but I could tell she'd lost Justine after only a few minutes.

I cleared my throat and Rosa took the hint. "Well, I'd better skedaddle, ladies. Lots of tidying up to do before my big trip. I'm going to Italy, you know." She scurried out of the door and into the hallway.

I turned back to Justine. "Sorry about that. Where were we?"

"Oh, I was telling you about the outdoor ceremony. A friend of Harold's works at the planetarium in Houston. He's going to loan us a telescope for the gazebo."

"Wow, that's awesome. Do I need to contact him or are you guys taking care of that?"

"We'll handle it. Anyway, people can star gaze, as I said, but those won't be the only stars they see. The idea is to have stars everywhere. Like, literally everywhere. Lots of glittering stars hanging from the trees. Snowflakes hanging from trees, too. Twinkling Christmas lights everywhere. The entire Club Wed facility could be lit up, including all of the trees on the property. It'll be a Christmas Wonderland." She paused and then snapped her fingers. "Oh, I've got it! Maybe we could even bring in some snow. What do you think of that idea?"

"It'd be a first for Club Wed." I offered a strained smile and wrote down the words: "Bring in snow. Hmm." Still, I couldn't help but wonder: Wouldn't it melt if the temps were in the sixties?

Justine rose and paced the room, the animation level in her voice rising. "And just you wait. The station will want to film the whole thing, so Club Wed will end up on the evening news." She glanced my way and offered a little shrug. "Not that you guys need more business, of course. Anyone who's anyone is getting married at Club Wed these days."

"Since you brought that up, I should tell you that we've opened a new facility in Splendora and things are going well there, too. Maybe we could focus our attention on sending prospective brides to that facility?"

"Splendora?" Justine laughed. "Of all the towns you could have chosen, why Splendora?"

"Kind of a funny story, actually. We have friends there. Lots and lots of friends. So, I'm looking at asking some of them to get involved in the process. The last time we talked you mentioned needing singers for the reception?"

"Yes. You know someone?"

"Several someones. I'd like to recommend some ladies from Splendora who will do a fine job."

I'd just started to tell her about Twila, Bonnie Sue and Jolene—my three quirky golden-years friends—when a knock at the door interrupted us. I glanced over as my sister-in-law, Scarlet, stuck her head inside.

"Sorry I'm late." She released an exaggerated sigh. "You wouldn't believe the day I've had."

I cut her off with the words, "No problem" before she could dive into an explanation. No doubt we'd be here all day, otherwise.

She took a couple of steps into the office and plopped down into the chair Justine had just been sitting in. "What did I miss? Please don't tell me you've designed the cake without me."

"Heavens, no." Justine giggled and her cheeks turned pink. "Get it? Heavens?"

Scarlet squinted her eyes, clearly not understanding Justine's little play on words.

"We haven't talked about the cake yet," I assured her. My gaze shifted to her *Let Them Eat Cake* apron, which was covered in chocolate frosting. And some sort of green sugary blobs.

"Ooh, you smell yummy. Sugar!" Justine's eyes widened as she glanced Scarlet's way.

"Oh, good grief. Can't believe I forgot to take this off." Scarlet scrambled to pull off the apron, revealing a dark blouse underneath. It, too, had the markings of some sort of sugary substance. Powdered sugar, perhaps? Yep. As Scarlet settled into the chair, a plume of white powder puffed around her. Reminded me of Charlie Brown's friend, Pig Pen. Only, not.

"Some pro I am." Scarlet laughed as she folded her apron. "I hope you'll forgive me, Justine. I'm in the middle of a baking extravaganza. Making a couple of birthday cakes for Bella's twins."

Justine looked my way. "Bella? The twins are already a year old? I thought they were younger."

"Not until next month," I explained. "But my aunt and

uncle are leaving the country on holiday and we had to rush the party to this weekend. We're racing toward the goal and Scarlet's been kind enough to help. We wouldn't get our cakes from anyone else."

"It's Elsa and Anna." Scarlet paused and giggled. "That's the theme of the party, not the names of the kids. Elsa and Anna are characters from—"

"Frozen! My favorite movie!" Justine dove into a lengthy explanation about why Frozen was the perfect movie for a meteorologist.

Scarlet chimed in with her thoughts and before long the two ladies had obviously forgotten I was still in the room. I managed to catch Scarlet's eye and she quieted down in a hurry. "Sorry. I just get so excited."

"I'm glad you do!" Justine giggled. "I hope you're just as excited about my cake."

"Are you kidding? This is going to be the best ever." Scarlet reached across my desk and grabbed a notepad and pen. "Let's get busy designing, girl."

"Mm-hmm." Justine's eyes sparkled and she took a seat in the chair next to Scarlet. "I'm so glad Bella recommended you."

"Thanks. Happy to be of service." Scarlet twirled the pen around in her fingers. "So, what are you thinking, cake-wise? I've had you on the calendar for months but it's time to hyper-focus on design, so be specific."

"Ooh, I want it to be tiered, of course."

"Right. But, fondant or buttercream?"

"She makes a yummy cream cheese frosting," I threw in. "Best in town."

"Don't tell Rosa that." Scarlet glanced toward the door, as if expecting my aunt to sneak back in unannounced.

"Mmm. Love cream cheese." Justine licked her lips. "And white cakes with some sort of heavenly filling that's cloud-like. Marshmallow, maybe? Too sticky? Too sweet?"

"Maybe. Probably Italian buttercream. It's light as a feather." Scarlet wrinkled her nose and mouthed the words "Heavenly filling" as she wrote them down.

"Lots of layers would be great," Justine added. "Like, really, really tall. Super-tall. Sort of a 'reaching to the heavens' look? And sparkly. Like snow. Only, not really. Maybe sugar crystals? Something heavenly. And speaking of the heavens…"

"Yes?" Scarlet looked up from her scribbling.

"I was thinking shimmering stars." Justine gestured with her hand in a sweeping motion. "All over the cake. Maybe even sticking out of the cake on wires. Like they're floating above it. Can you do that? Float stars, I mean?"

"Of course! I love a good challenge." Scarlet sat up straight in her chair. "Fondant stars? Gum paste? Isomalt?"

"Whatever you think. You're the baker. Ooh, and speaking of stars, can you do some gorgeous sugar cookies that look like stars? Really detailed, I mean."

"Yep. Royal icing. Lots of sanding sugar." Scarlet scribbled faster and faster. "Star cookies. Got it."

"And maybe some crescent moon shaped ones, too. And snowflakes. Can you do snowflake cookies? Cover them in something shimmery?"

"Yep. Love it." Scarlet continued to scribble.

I sat back in my chair and let the ladies do their thing. Soon enough they'd involve me again. The conversation eventually shifted to the foods we would be providing for the wedding. Star shaped pasta, covered in Rosa's yummy Alfredo sauce, garlic crescent rolls, melon and sandwiches, cut to look like stars, and so on. My thoughts reeled back to Aunt Rosa and I prayed she would arrive back from her trip feeling strong enough to help with the wedding foods. Heaven help us if she didn't. My poor brother Nick would have his work cut out for him.

Just as we wrapped up the conversation about the foods, Justine looked my way. "Now, Bella, I don't want to scare you, but it's liable to be chaotic at the wedding. We've got a ton of people coming from the network. Lots of reporters and even the mayor of Houston. A couple of players from the Astros and even a big-wig from the astronomy department at Rice University. He's Harold's best friend. All in all it'll be quite an eclectic bunch."

"Sounds like it." We would have to put our best foot forward. Then again, we'd managed to impress plenty of well-known Hollywood-types in the past; surely we could do it again.

"Science people, artsy folks and family, all merged into one room." Justine's eyes took on a far-away look. "I guess that's what my new normal is going to look like, now that I'm marrying a science guy."

"You're sciency too, though," I said.

"More artsy.' She pointed at her outfit. "I don't know if you ever watch me do the weather, but I try to mix it up. Take a creative slant. I don't play anything straight, which is why they hired me. I've even been known to sing the weather forecast." She giggled. "It's my theater background."

Yep. This would be a theatrical production, no doubt about it. Still, as I pondered the weathergirl's plans, as I tried to envision snowflakes, stars and twinkling lights, I had to admit. . .it all sounded rather magical.

Chapter Three

NIGHT AND DAY

"Weather forecast for tonight: dark." — George Carlin

After meeting with Justine at Club Wed, I picked up the kiddos from my parents' house next door and headed home to Casa de la Neeley, my place of refuge. In the years since D.J. and I had become Mr. and Mrs., this house had become a home. First, for the two of us. Then, along came Tres and little Rosie. Then, the twins.

Now the old Victorian stood, not as a testament to my husband's amazing carpentry skills, not a nod to my love of decorating, but a tribute to our rowdy family of six.

Hmm. Family of six. If anyone had told this little Italian girl that she'd end up married to an east Texas cowboy from Splendora Texas with four rambunctious children, she would've said they were nuts. Having been raised in a large family, I knew the drawbacks, but I also knew the joys. Now, I had to confess: the more, the merrier.

Not that we were planning to have more. Um, no. I barely had arms enough to carry the four I had, at least for now.

I trudged up the front steps with Holly on one hip and

Ivy on the other, Rosie tugging at the hem of my blouse and Tres tagging behind us, playing a game on my phone. The phone rang just as I stuck the key in the front door. No point in bothering to answer it now, not with my arms so full.

Tres took care of that for me. I heard his cheerful, "Hello?" from behind me just as I stepped inside, followed by, "Mama, phone!"

I set the twins into their pack-and-play in the corner of the living room and reached for the phone, unsure of who I'd find on the other end of the line.

"Hey, girl."

Ah. Scarlet.

"I just wanted to double-check something. How many guests at the Collins wedding? Two- fifty?"

"More like three-fifty." I glanced at the front door, realizing I'd left it wide open. "It's going to be a tight squeeze, getting everyone inside the reception hall, and don't even get me started on how we're going to fit that many chairs in the gazebo area. But these two are very popular." My purse slid off of my shoulder and bumped Rosie in the head. She let out a cry and I knelt down to kiss her and make it better.

Tres raced across the living room and dove into a pile of toy trucks. Rosie dried her eyes and followed behind him.

"I didn't realize what a big deal the bride and groom were until I mentioned the wedding to my grandmother." Scarlet said. "Apparently the fiancé has a real following and the bride was listed as one of the Top Ten Most Influential Females in Texas. Did you have any idea?"

"Yeah, I did. It's going to be a doozie of a night, that's for sure. And we need to be on the lookout for media types." I took a seat on the sofa, keeping a watchful eye on the four kids.

"Paparazzi? Scarlet giggled. "You really think they'll show up?"

"Girl, you weren't here when Brock Benson was best man in a wedding I coordinated. We had paparazzi in force." I kicked off my shoes and stretched my feet, happy for a moment or relaxation. Well, until Rosie started crying because Tres wouldn't share his trucks with her.

"Well, yeah, that's Brock Benson, though," Scarlet said. "He's famous. Hollywood star, and all that. But, a local weather girl and a geeky science guy? I guess I just hadn't considered them stars." She giggled. "See what I did there? Stars?" Another laugh followed.

"We just need to be prepared. That's all I'm saying. Maybe I'm worrying for nothing, but you never know. Sometimes my worries are a prediction that something's going to happen."

"Predictions?" She laughed. "I see what you did. But you're no weather girl, Bella. I wouldn't place too much stock in those predictions. . .er, worries."

Rosie let out a loud squeal and I looked up to discover D.J. had entered the house. One look at my handsome husband—those gorgeous twinkling eyes, the broad shoulders, the messy blonde hair, and I felt like swooning. Not much had changed over the years. The guy still took my breath away.

He gave me a "Hang up the phone and come give me a kiss" look and I felt my cheeks growing warm. "Um, Scarlet? I have to go."

"Yeah, me too. Armando's taking me out to dinner. Sounds like we'll be doing a lot of that once Rosa and Laz leave."

"Have fun."

I ended the call and set the cell phone down on the coffee

table, right next to a couple of stuffed animals and a Tonka truck. As I rose and stretched my back, D.J. opened his arms. . .an invitation. I took several steps his way, finally leaning in to him, comfortable in his loving embrace. A few sweet kisses in my hair and then his lips met mine for a lingering kiss.

"Daddy! Daddy!" Rosie called out and D.J. swept her into his arms. The three of us stood together until Tres joined us, the party growing to four. From across the room the twins squealed with glee from inside their pack-and-play. In that moment, the most delicious feeling swept over me. Every dream I'd ever dreamed had come true, and all because God had blessed me with the perfect-for-me-guy.

My thoughts reeled back in time. I'd fallen in love with my husband, D.J., the minute I saw him. Our meeting didn't have anything to do with the sun, the moon or the stars. It had everything to do with a huge misunderstanding. I thought I was hiring a deejay for a wedding. Turned out, a handsome east Texas cowboy named D.J. ambled his way into my heart. . .and nothing had been the same since.

My honey kept a watchful eye on the kiddos while I prepped dinner—a salad and my favorite soup, Pasta Fagioli. We managed to get through the meal and bathe the kids, all-the-while talking about the upcoming wedding. By the time we settled into bed, exhausted from our evening ritual, I had a feeling D.J. would rather watch a show than listen to me ramble on about a celestial-themed ceremony, but he humored me anyway.

"Okay, D.J., here's the thing." I opened my laptop and searched for the file for the Collins wedding. "I really need your help. With the whole starry night theme, they've asked something special regarding the song list. Armando will act as deejay, but he's not going to be very helpful choosing the kind of music we're talking about. It's out of his element."

"Okay. Shoot."

"The only thing we'll be shooting is stars," I explained with a playful wink.

"Say what?" My hubby gave me a curious look and leaned back against his pillows. I found myself momentarily distracted by him—that chiseled physique, the abs of steel—hard-earned from his work in construction. Mmm. Any girl with half a brain would toss the laptop over the side of the bed and forget about working.

"What were you saying, honey?" D.J.'s words caused me to snap to attention.

"Hmm? Oh, they've asked that every song have the word sun, moon or stars in it. Well, that, or something to do with the weather. Like stormy weather."

"Stormy Weather?" He pulled the blanket over his legs. "Not much of a wedding song."

"Right, and that's half the problem. Justine put together a list of meteorologist-approved tunes, but half of them don't have the romance angle. They're gonna be hard to dance to."

"So...." He yawned. "I'm supposed to be on the lookout for shooting star songs?"

"With the appropriate romantic angle, if you don't mind."

"Right. Romantic." He quirked a brow and gave me a 'come hither' look. I shifted my focus back to the computer. "I'm just so panicked about getting all of this done in time. With Rosa and Laz gone. . ." My words drifted off as my enthusiasm waned.

"Why are you so bugged about Rosa and Laz going away?" D.J. asked. "If anyone deserves a break, they do."

"Right. I guess I just. . ." I released a slow, exaggerated

breath. "I don't like change, D.J. I'm a creature of habit."

"Meaning?"

"Meaning, it feels good to know that, day in and day out, the people I love are always right there at my side. We're a team. You know? And it's just not the same when some of the team members are missing."

He paused and I wished I could read his thoughts.

"I'm still saying Rosa and Laz need time away," D.J. said at last. "To rediscover each other. Spend time with just the two of them. It's important to their marriage. You know?"

Uh-oh. Now we weren't talking about Rosa and Laz anymore, were we?

I set my laptop aside, leaned over and gave D.J. a little peck on the cheek. He pulled me close and kissed me soundly. "We need a vacation, too, Bella-bambina," he said, his words soft and inviting.

I couldn't help but smile as he called me by the nickname.

"A vacation?" Hmm. Sounded lovely. Unrealistic, but lovely.

His lips traveled down my neck and onto my shoulder, then met my lips once again, the kiss deepening in intensity.

Oh my. Who needed to work? Not this girl.

From the other room, I heard one of the twins let out a cry. I ignored it. Then the other twin joined in.

D.J. stopped kissing me and gave a little shrug. "I'll make you a deal." He swung his legs over the edge of the bed. "You look up star songs and I'll take care of Holly and Ivy."

Alrighty then. "You've got a deal." I gave him a little wink, convinced I could handle this. I scoured my search engine and before long found myself lost in a sea of starsongs. Well, until D.J. showed back up with Holly in his arms.

"She wants Mommy." He set her on the bed between us and I gazed into her eyes, still moist from crying. "Do you mind?"

"Of course not."

Holly bounced my way with an exuberant "Mama, Mama, Mama!"

Time to close the laptop.

I might be a working mother, but right now I just needed to be a mama. Stifling a yawn, I opted to lean back against the pillows. As I cradled my daughter in my arms, a dizzying haze settled over me, a foggy coma-like state. I couldn't move if I wanted to, not with exhaustion now eking out of every pore. Instead, I allowed my eyes to flutter closed and drifted, drifted, drifted off to dreamland.

Chapter Four

FULL MOON AND EMPTY ARMS

"But who wants to be foretold the weather? It is bad enough when it comes, without our having the misery of knowing about it beforehand." — Jerome K. Jerome

When an Italian family member plans a trip to the Old Country—aka Italy—the entire family gets involved. For instance, I don't think Rosa even got to pick out which under-garments she wanted to pack. Mama insisted on a shopping spree to Houston, where she helped Rosa select all new unmentionables. Not that anyone in the Rossi family considered anything "unmentionable" – or private, for that matter.

The visit to Houston's famous Galleria consisted of women hovering around the satin and nylon panties, oohing and aahing over the various cuts and colors. This, according to my younger sister, Sophia, who seemed a little creeped out by the adventure, especially when Mama insisted on a new negligee in a lovely shade of red for our elderly aunt.

"Can you even picture Aunt Rosa wearing that?" Sophia whispered as we gathered on the veranda that final Saturday in November to see Rosa and Laz off on their journey. "Rosa? In a sexy red nightie? Ick!"

A shiver wriggled its way down my spine. Might've had something to do with the weather. We were experiencing a drop in temperatures, as Justine so aptly called it. A cold front. Or maybe the shiver had more to do with Sophia's comment. I certainly didn't want to picture my aunt and uncle in their bedclothes—or lack thereof—any more than I wanted to imagine my parents being intimate. Gross. I pinched my eyes shut to avoid thinking about it.

Then again, if the older folks had never been intimate, none of us would exist, so maybe I'd better get over it. I opened my eyes just in time to see the front door of the Rossi home swing open. Laz and Rosa bounded out, one after the other, followed by my three brothers, who all lugged large expensive suitcases, heavy numbers that looked indestructible.

"They got new luggage, too?" I asked. "Those new Tumi bags must've set Laz back a ton."

"The Food Network sent them as a gift," Sophia explained.

"For Christmas, you mean?" Surely they weren't meant to be a retirement gift. . .right? Someone would've told me if Rosa and Laz were thinking about quitting their show.

"I dunno." Sophia must've been thinking along the same lines. She leaned my way to whisper the next part. "I can't picture either of them ever retiring. You heard that their producer turned this whole month-long trip to Italy into a work project? They've been commissioned to photograph their favorite foods and interview cooks along the way. They're traveling with a cameraman."

"No way." Maybe I should've been bothered by that news—after all, Rosa and Laz deserved their privacy—but it brought some degree of comfort to know that they weren't planning to give up their show any time soon. Breaking with tradition was hard. Very hard.

"Yeah, but look on the bright side. The trip is now being funded by the network, right down to the expensive luggage." She pointed at the Tumi bags. "There are worse gigs, I suppose."

"Still, to never be able to break away from your work? To only ever go around the clock, even during a season like Christmas, when you'd hoped to spend time with your family?"

Oh. Ouch. Suddenly I wasn't concerned about Rosa and Laz anymore. I thought about D.J.'s admonition that I worked too hard. Put in too many hours. Spent my "at home" hours focused on weddings and not on the things that mattered.

Looked like I came from a long line of over-achievers. People who didn't know how to say no.

I refocused my attention on Laz, who gave Nick, Joey and D.J. instructions for how to maneuver the bags down the front steps. For the first time I noticed my uncle wore the strangest get-up: plaid pants that looked pajama-like, and an overly casual t-shirt. Rosa grumbled at him as he fastened a nametag on one of the suitcases.

"I asked you to change into something decent," she said.

"I'm out of bed and dressed," he grumbled. "What more do you want?"

"I'm just saying you could have put a little more thought into what you're wearing, that's all."

"I put a lot of thought into it. We're going to be on a plane for fourteen hours and I want to be comfortable." He released his hold on the luggage tag and flashed a smile as he spoke to the whole group of us. "Speaking of comfortable, did you hear that the Food Network got us seating in First Class? We'll be in a pod."

"A pod?" Pop looked confused by this.

"Yes. I saw pictures online. It's the strangest thing, but the seats are in little private areas that look like pods."

"I just hope they're putting you on an airplane and not an alien spaceship." My father laughed and reached for one of the bags. "Better double-check that pod before you climb into it, Laz."

My uncle promised to do just that.

Still, I couldn't have put it any better: two peas in a pod. Rosa and Laz. Perfect description of the two of them.

From inside the house I heard Guido—the family's colorful parrot—crooning a Frank Sinatra tune. *My Way*. Wow. I'd never heard him attempt that one before. Must be Rosa's influence. Laz must've heard it too. He stopped in his tracks, glanced back at the door and sighed.

"Do me a favor, Imelda." He reached to give my mother's hand a squeeze. "Give that bird a steady dose of Dean Martin songs while we're gone. I'd like to see him reformed by the time I get home."

"Didn't we try to reform Guido once before?" Pop asked.

True, that. When Guido first arrived at the Rossi home, he cursed like a sailor. Laz's attempts to train the bird in the ways of the Lord had failed miserably. Well, mostly. Guido had mastered a few scriptures, but always seemed to mix them up with a warbling rendition of *100 Bottles of Beer on the Wall*. At least he'd conquered *That's Amore*.

"Yes, well. . .At any rate, promise you'll take good care of my Guido." Laz's eyes misted over. "Feed him every morning and don't forget his allergy meds. If you skip a dose, he's liable to lose his feathers again. Oh, and remember, we just had his wings clipped."

"We'll do fine, Laz." Mama rolled her eyes. I knew her

take on that bird. She'd rather not have him in the house. Still, putting him outdoors would never do, especially during the winter season. The poor fella's beak would freeze shut.

On the other hand, my mother would probably like that proposition. At least the little guy wouldn't drive her crazy singing all day.

Ah well. I would ease her mind by taking Guido to Club Wed. He loved it there.

"Oh, I know you love Guido too, and will take great care of him." Laz's eyes misted over. "Just don't want you to forget that he needs a balanced diet of veggies, grains, seeds, nuts, fruits. . .all the things we love, basically. Nothing processed. Nothing high in sugar or fat."

"So none of that tiramisu I left in the fridge." Rosa laughed.

"Rosa, have I ever given that bird anything with sugar in it?" Mama rolled her eyes. "Why would I start now? Surely you two know that you can trust me with Guido. I haven't killed him yet."

"It's just that I'm usually the one to take care of him," Laz said. "So I've left a detailed list. A little birdseed is fine, but not too much. He likes fruit best. And nectar."

"Nectar?" Pop asked. "Should I give him a swig of my Christmas brandy?"

"Cosmo!" Rosa fanned herself. "Guido does not do well with mind-altering remedies. Remember that time we gave him an antihistamine? It made him loopy."

I remembered that day well. Guido had almost ruined a perfectly lovely wedding rehearsal that night by stealing a guest's toupee. Never. Again.

We all followed behind them to the car. Nick, their chauffeur for the day, led the way, luggage in hand. God bless that brother of mine for being willing to go so far out of his way for family.

Then again, that's how it was in the Rossi household. Going out of one's way was just the way of it. . .and I wouldn't change a thing.

Rosa looked on as the men loaded her luggage in the trunk of the vehicle, then glanced our way, her eyes flooded with tears. "Ooh, I'm going to miss you all so much."

"No you won't," Laz countered. "You're going to be too busy to miss anyone." He quirked a brow and pictures of that red negligee skittered through my brain. Gross. I scrub-brushed my thoughts and refocused.

Rosa kissed us all on the cheeks, then gave Mama the biggest hug of all. "I'll post our pictures on Facebook so you can keep up with us."

"Facebook?" Laz grunted, then mumbled something about how social media would be the death of them. He gestured for my brothers to bring their bags down the front steps of the veranda. Nick and Joey did fine with theirs, but D.J. struggled with the largest bag. One of them took off like it had a mind of its own, tumbling down the steps. He caught it just before catastrophe struck.

"Easy there, cowboy." Laz patted my husband on the shoulder. "There are some mighty fine new things in that bag. My sweetie went shopping, you see."

Ew.

"Let's go back to the Facebook comment." Rosa offered a little pout. "Now Laz, be serious. You know our viewers will expect us to post photos every step of the way. I plan to do just that. And you know we'll have to tweet, too."

"Tweet?" Another grunt followed from Uncle Laz. "The only tweeting I do is after eating Brussels sprouts, but I don't plan to have any of those on this trip." He gave her a little wink and then slung his arm over her shoulder as she groaned aloud.

Rosa began to hum *That's Life*, her favorite Sinatra tune—and the theme song for Brock Benson's new sitcom. Uncle Laz's gaze narrowed, and for a moment I thought he might counter with a Dean Martin song. Strange. I thought my aunt and uncle had ended their ongoing feud over which was the better singer—Old Blue Eyes or Deano. I had my preference, but knew better than to state it aloud.

I watched as Nick helped them into the backseat. He'd just come off of a late shift at Parma John's the night before and must be exhausted. I could read the weariness in his eyes. Still, he'd willingly volunteered to transport the happy travelers to the airport. Hard working guy. Hmm. More proof that I came by it honestly.

My gaze shifted to Club Wed next door. The expansive old Victorian loomed like a beacon in the night, calling my name. It had a Pied Piper quality about it, which sucked me in, whether I felt like working or not. Today, on my day off, I knew I should avoid the place, especially since D.J. and the kids were keen on going to Moody Gardens to see the holiday decorations. Still, it wouldn't hurt to stop by the office for just a minute to check on something.

As we waved goodbye to my aunt and uncle, I turned to my hubby, braving the question. "D.J., would you mind watching the kids for a minute or two? I need to check on something in my office. Make sure I don't have any messages on the machine. Won't take long."

He gave me that look I'd grown accustomed to. I recognized it as the same look my mother used to give me whenever she wanted to scold but chose to bite her tongue, instead.

"I'll just be a minute, I promise."

The minute turned into about twenty minutes. I couldn't help myself, really. One voice mail led to another, one email message led to the next, and before long I was talking to one of our vendors.

I'd totally lost myself in the moment when I heard a familiar cry. Rosie. Looking up, I noticed D.J. standing in the door. "Bella?" His wrinkled brow clued me in to the fact that he wasn't particularly happy with me. "You're still working?"

"What time is it?"

"Ten minutes till one. The kids are starving. We were going to have lunch at Parma Johns before heading to Moody Gardens, right?"

"Right." I slapped myself on the forehead. "D.J., I'm sorry. I don't know what comes over me. It's like. . ."

"Someone puts a spell on you."

"Yeah, I guess." I gestured to my office. "It's this place. It has that effect on me."

"Then let's get out of here before it pulls you through the looking glass, okay? I'm so hungry, I could eat a whole sausage pizza by myself."

As we headed outside, the skies overhead hovered with their dismal gray clouds. Uh oh. A strong wind drifted in from the south, blowing the leaves from the trees in the front yard. Rosie began to cry, but Tres greeted it as an opportunity. He ran across the yard, chasing the leaves and squealing with childish delight. In that moment, I was struck by a thought that must have come from heaven on high. Even with a storm blowing around us, Tres' carefree attitude made me feel like a kid again. I wanted to toss my cares—and my work—to the wind and just play.

I couldn't help but think that I had a few lessons to learn from my son. What I needed was a new perspective. Eyes to see the winds the way my little boy did. If I could manage that, perhaps I could relax a little. Re-learn how to rest. And while I was at it, I might just get to watch the tension unfold itself from my husband's wrinkled forehead.

Chapter Five

SHAKE DOWN THE STARS

"In my opinion, too much attention to weather makes for instability of character." —Elizabeth Goudge

There are those rare people in your world who sparkle and shine above and beyond the norm. They rush in like a mighty wind and whirl around you with such verbosity that you wonder how much you can take. But they glisten with such an effervescent shimmer that you know—in spite of their wackiness—that you would sooner die than try to live without them.

Such was the case with the Splendora sisters.

I'd met Twila, Jolene and Bonnie Sue years earlier at a charismatic church in the tiny town Splendora, miles north of Houston. The three plus-sized divas made a vivid first impression as they worshipped up and down the aisle, three buxom Tammy Fayes, complete with the eyelashes and tattooed lip liner. Being raised a Methodist I'd never witnessed such vibrant displays of worship before. Or seen that particular shade of eye shadow. And the glittery blouses, along with the upswept hairdos and strategically placed hair clips, made me wonder if, perhaps, I'd ventured onto a movie set instead of a local church. Still, one couldn't help but be drawn in. I couldn't take my eyes off of them that first night, and now—years later—they still drew my attention every time they showed up on the island.

I laid aside my pre-conceived ideas as soon as I got to know them. Twila won me over with her charm and her heart for the Lord. Well, that, and her remarkable makeup tips. Who knew that you could use hemorrhoid cream to get rid of wrinkles? Amazing revelation. My mother still lathered up before she went to bed at night, thanks to Twila.

The three God-fearin' gals wormed their way into the hearts of my family members and the whole of Galveston, alongside them. We always saw the ladies more often during the holidays because they sang at our local Dickens on the Strand event. The mayor always made a big to-do over them. And why not? Their harmonies were legendary, and they put on quite a show for viewers, with over-the-top choreography and snappy rhythms.

With all of this in mind, I decided to take matters into my own hands and include them in Justine's wedding plans. She would love these gals. No doubt about it. And her guests would, too. In fact, this might just take the Splendora trio's fame to new heights, what with Houston's mayor showing up. Perhaps they'd get more gigs out of it.

On the first Thursday in December, just a little more than two weeks shy of Justine's big day, the Splendora sisters blew into Club Wed like an incoming hurricane. I had issued the invitation knowing Justine was still looking for entertainment for her reception. Still, I had to laugh when I saw their Victorian gowns and feathered hats.

"You're singing tonight at Dickens on the Strand?" I asked.

"What was your first guess?" Twila primped a bit and laughed.

"Love that burgundy dress on you, Twila." I let out a little whistle. "You're as pretty as a Victorian postcard."

"And nearly as old." She gave me a wink. "Kidding, kidding. But I'm feeling my age with the weather changing so much. Just about the time my hip joints unlock from the cold, it turns hot again and they slip out of place."

"We're in Texas, Twila. What do you expect? If you don't like the weather, just hang on a minute. It'll change." Bonnie Sue doubled over with laughter. "Oh, that's rich."

"Speaking of rich, did you taste those chocolate truffles in the foyer? I nabbed one on the way in. Hope that's okay, Bella."

"Of course. I put them there for guests." Not that these gals were guests. They were family. And, as I ushered them into my office, I hoped to make them Justine's family, as well. We'd start with proper introductions.

Justine looked up as we entered, her eyes widening as she took in the Victorian costumes. "What have we here?"

"Friends from Splendora," I said. I turned my attention to the trio. "Ladies, I've invited you here today to meet a new bride, Justine." I gestured to the lovely bride-to-be and Twila gasped. She reached with a plump hand for a Club Wed brochure from my desk and began to fan herself. "Why, I'd know that lovely face anywhere."

"Ooh, me too." Bonnie Sue leaned in close to Justine, whose eyes widened. "I never forget a face. We've seen you. . .somewhere."

"She's a movie star!" Jolene plopped down into the seat next to Justine and reached with a fingertip to brush a loose hair from her face. "Tell me I'm right. No, I know! You're in

Brock Benson's TV show, right? The one about the Greek gyro shop? I know Bella has been helping the producers. You must be one of the actresses, am I right? Oh, I can see why they hired you. You have the loveliest pores. And that eyeliner job is spectacular. Where did you have it done?"

"Eyeliner job?" Justine squirmed in her seat. "I'm not in a sitcom, though I do feel a bit like I'm in one right now." She offered a faint smile. "But it's likely you have seen me on TV. I'm on every night on the—"

"I know! I know!" Bonnie Sue let out a squeal. "You're that beautiful blonde on *Wheel of Fortune*. Vanna something? Ooh, I just love that show. I've always been head-over-heels for the host, Bob Barker. Quite a sexy old guy, if I do say so, myself." She fanned her face with her hand. "And you haven't aged a bit, not one little bit. But don't you ever get tired of flipping all of those letters around? I mean, a job's a job, and you sure get to wear some pretty clothes and all, but just standing there, day after day, flipping letters? It has to get old."

"Justine doesn't work on *Wheel of Fortune*, Bonnie Sue." Twila rose and took a couple of steps in Justine's direction. "And Bob Barker hosted *The Price is Right,* so get your facts straight. This is that precious weather gal from Channel Eleven. The one who took over after the real weather guy—the one from the National Hurricane Center—left."

Oh. Ouch. I stared at Justine, who flinched. Ack.

"Justine is a trained meteorologist," I said. "Her predictions are spot on."

"Oh, please forgive me if I over-spoke. I was just so enamored with that older fellow who used to do the weather. So trustworthy. It was almost like he had a direct line to the Almighty, who fed him information on the sly about upcoming weather problems. You know?" Twila took Justine by the hand. "I would imagine that any weather person would have to have the Lord on speed-dial, wouldn't you?"

Justine looked perplexed by this notion. "Well, I never really thought about it much, to be honest."

"Ooh, you must think about it. He's the one who controls the weather, wouldn't you agree? So, you have to have a lifeline to the One making the decisions, especially in your line of work."

"I. . .I suppose."

"He hung the sun, the moon and the stars in place. And He knows every cloud in the sky...moves 'em around at his good pleasure." Bonnie Sue interjected. "He's your real boss, girlie, so if you haven't asked him to take on that role in your life, you might want to consider it."

"No offense, ladies, but I studied weather systems. I know how it works. There's a cause and effect reason for everything. Scientific explanations. You know?"

"Gobblety-gook." Twila waved her hand in the air. "Of course, there are scientific explanations for everything. But you can't science away the Lord, honey. He created all of it and He determines when the sun rises and sets, when and how the stars twinkle in the sky. . .every little old thing! He's in charge of it all."

"R-right." Justine shrugged and shot me a "How do I get out of this?" look.

"I suppose if the weather didn't change, half the people I know wouldn't have a thing to talk about. I've never heard so much senseless chatter about wind and rain." Bonnie Sue clamped a hand over her mouth and her cheeks flamed pink. "Oh, I'm sorry, Justine. Didn't mean to rain on your parade." When she realized what she'd said, she busted out laughing.

"Well, cut off my legs and call me shorty. I just can't seem to keep my foot out of my mouth today. I simply meant to say that weather is your business and I didn't mean to make light of it."

This somehow led to a discussion about a storm the ladies had experienced while onboard a cruise ship. I remembered that particular tropical storm well. In fact, I'd spent that night hunkered down in the foyer of the Rossi home, along with the people I loved.

"Ain't nothin' like a life-threatening storm to teach you just how much you're loved," Jolene said. "Folks trying to get in touch with their loved ones, doing what they can to make sure everyone they care about is okay."

"Never thought about that before," I said. "But you're right. On stormy days I just want to hear DJ's voice. And I call Sophia to talk to the kids, too. I miss them on rainy days, for sure."

"Rainy days were made for cuddling." Twila gave me a knowing look. "And for makin' babies."

"Twila!" Bonnie Sue whacked her on the back. "That's nobody's business."

"I'm just saying, lots of babies get their start on rainy days." Twila looked Justine's way. "Now *there's* a scientific fact for you. Look it up on the Internet. You'll see I'm right."

For whatever reason, all three Splendora sisters—and Justine—looked my way. I put my hands up in the air. "Oh no. I don't know if there's rain in the forecast or not, but even if there is it doesn't mean more babies are coming. We've got four little tornados already."

"You never know." Justine's eye's twinkled. "These ladies might be on to something. Ain't nothin' like a storm to broaden the family tree."

At this point the ladies decided to hold an audition. They broke into a rendition of *Stormy Weather* in perfect three-part harmony. Justine looked on, eyes twinkling with merriment. They followed this song with another, *Blue Skies*. I had to admit, they really sounded good.

When they ended, Justine clapped and let out a squeal. "Ooh, this is perfect. You're hired. You'll be great at the reception. Are you free on the night of the 19th, ladies?"

"Bella already asked," Twila said. "And yes we are. We'd be happy to sing at your wedding reception. From what Bella's told us, it's going to be a night to remember."

"Oh, I hope so." Justine sighed. "Everything's coming together so beautifully." She paused for a moment and her smile seemed to fade.

"Something wrong?" I asked, concern overtaking me.

"Oh, just thinking about a little family situation we're facing. You know how it is at weddings, Bella. There are always a few folks you'd rather leave off the invitation list." Her eyes filled with tears, my first clue that we might be in for a real problem.

"Justine? Is everything okay?" I asked.

"What is it, honey?" Jolene rested her hand on Justine's arm. "You can tell us."

She sighed and took a seat. "I hate to complain, especially to total strangers."

"We're not strangers," Twila took a seat next to her. "We're one big happy family. At least we will be, by the time the wedding is over. So, what's happening? How can we help?"

Justine's gaze traveled to the floor. "I thought this whole wedding thing would be easier, but I was wrong."

"What's happened?" I asked, my heart rate increasing.

"It's so dumb. My dad—have I mentioned my parents are divorced?—anyway, my dad wants to bring his fiancée to the wedding. Well, actually, they'll be married by then. They're running off to Vegas week after next. But my mom is flipping out, and I don't really blame her. I mean, it's only been three months since my parents' divorce, and my dad left my mother for the woman he's now engaged to. It's going to be so hard on my mom to have Didi there."

"What about you?" Twila asked.

"What do you mean?"

"I mean, it's important that you be comfortable," Twila said, her voice soothing. "What's going to be the best—and easiest—thing for you?"

Justine rose and paced the tiny office, finally turning back to face us. "I just need—want—everyone to play nice, and that's going to be easier if Didi isn't there. She's a piece of work, for sure. And I know she'll go out of her way to make my mom feel uncomfortable. And if my mom's uncomfortable then I'll be uncomfortable, which kind of ruins the whole day." Justine groaned. "Why is this so hard? You would think someone who predicts storms could weather a few in her own life."

Twila crossed her arms at her chest. "Problem is, you can't predict the outcome."

"What do you mean?"

"You're used to looking ahead and seeing how things are going to be with the weather, and when it comes to stuff like this—the situation with your parents and the other woman—you can't see the outcome."

"Never thought about that, but I guess you're right. Maybe I don't want to see what's coming with my dad. He's been so awful to my mom this past year. And I'll be honest. .

.he's been so unpredictable. All of this is out of character for him. There's no rhyme or reason to it. Irrational behavior, if you ask me. If Didi comes it'll be awful for everyone involved...except my dad and Didi, and even then I have to question her motives for wanting to be there."

"Then you have your answer," Twila said. "It's better if she doesn't come. You have to tell your dad that."

"Yeah." Justine sighed. "I'm not used to telling my dad what to do."

"But this is your special day, Justine, and you deserve to be at peace," Bonnie Sue rested her hand on Justine's shoulder. "That means, he has to play nice."

"Playing nice is not what he does, at least not lately."

"Then we'll pray that he sees things your way." Bonnie Sue smiled and clasped her hands together, as if heading into a prayer meeting at this very moment. If so, it wouldn't be the first time I'd seen the Splendora sisters in action. They were prayer warriors, for sure. Still, I wondered how Justine would respond.

The bride-to-be paused and looked at the three ladies, tiny wrinkles forming on her forehead. "You people talk a lot about praying."

"Yes Ma'am, we do." Twila gave her a serious look. "You know how you predict the weather?"

"Right." Justine nodded.

"We don't have the ability to predict what's coming next in the real world." Twila said. "So, we have to trust that God knows all of that. We pray and ask for his direction in the moment because we won't be able to know what to do, otherwise."

Sometimes I act like I have it all together, like I know what's coming, when—in reality—I'm just hoping. Guessing."

Justine shrugged. "Is that awful?"

Twila reached over to squeeze the bride-to-be's hand. "Promise me you'll think about what I said earlier, about asking the Lord to be your boss. You'll never regret that decision."

"I'll think about it, for sure." Justine, God bless her, gave Twila a bright smile followed by a nod. "And in the meantime, let's stop talking about Didi, if you don't mind? Let's switch to something pleasant. Something less destructive."

Everyone responded with a resounding, "Okay."

Justine's eyes sparkled. "Good. Now, I have a proposition for you ladies, one I think you'll love."

"Name it, kiddo." Twila put her hands on her ample hips and grinned. "What can we do for you?"

"I want to invite the three of you to sing *Stormy Weather* on the six o'clock news." A playful smile turned up the edges of Justine's lips. "My final day at work is on Friday night, December 11th. After that I have three weeks off for the wedding and honeymoon. Wouldn't it be just perfect—I mean, wouldn't it be great—if you ladies crooned a tune my final night on the job? It would be quite the send-off. People wouldn't forget it."

No, indeed, they would not. If the Splendora sisters appeared on the evening news, I had a feeling folks would be talking about it for years to come.

Chapter Six

POLKA DOTS AND MOONBEAMS

"The sun did not shine. It was too wet to play. So we sat in the house. All that cold, cold, wet day."
— Dr. Seuss, *The Cat in the Hat*

On the day after meeting with Justine and the Splendora sisters I dove back into my work. My ever-growing "to do" list kept me going all morning, but by early afternoon I needed a break. Mama and Sophia agreed to watch the kids so that I could spend a couple of hours at our local Wal-Mart looking at Christmas presents for the kids. With only three weeks until my favorite holiday—and a good chunk of that time taken up with wedding planning—I needed to be proactive.

I browsed the aisles, my thoughts tumbling. I wanted to focus on the kids. Of course I did. But with phone calls and text messages coming in from brides at such a rapid pace, who had time to think about Tonka trucks and La-La-Loopsy dolls?

Just as I landed on the electronics aisle, my phone rang again. I didn't recognize the number, but answered anyway.

"Is this Bella Neeley?" A young woman's voice greeted me.

"This is she." I shifted my phone to the other ear, my gaze shifting to a video game I knew Tres would love.

Unfortunately, it was locked away behind a sliding glass door. Hmm.

"My name is Victoria Brierley. I heard all about you from Gabi Delgado, the dress designer."

"Yes, I know Gabi. We're good friends."

"Awesome. She's designing a gown for me, as we speak. Anyway, she gave me your contact information. My fiancé Beau and I are getting married in February. We want to do sort of a Victorian tea-party theme. Get it?"

I didn't, but couldn't respond because a lady shoved past me with her cart, nearly knocking me down.

"My name's Victoria," the woman on the phone said. "And I want a Victorian wedding." A little giggle followed.

"Ah. Got it. Cute."

"Valentine's Day is on a Sunday, which is a weird day for a wedding, but I figured you guys might not be booked on a Sunday. . .so I thought I'd asked. Is Club Wed available?"

"We have a Saturday morning ceremony and a Saturday evening one, as well. Nothing on Sunday." *But boy, will my feet ever be killing me if I say Yes to you.*

"Oh, please say we can have that slot." She laughed. "I just have to get married at Club Wed. I went to your website and just fell in love with the place. And from what Gabi has told me, it's even better in person."

"Oh, it is," I said. "The pictures don't do it justice."

"I think it'll be great for Valentine's Day. So, go ahead and put our names down, okay? I'll mail you a deposit check."

A beep sounded from my phone, a text message coming through. I carried on with the conversation with Victoria, then ended the call. I pulled the phone away from my ear, glanced down and groaned as I read the incoming text message from Justine:

"You available to talk?" Really? I wanted to respond with: "I'm off the clock, girl." Instead, I opted with the obvious, "Call me." Which, she did.

We spent the next half hour talking about her concerns over the layout of the gazebo and chairs At some point I realized I'd been strolling the aisles of the toy department for ages without picking out one thing for the kids. I pulled the phone away from my ear and groaned when I saw the time: four o'clock. Had I been on the phone that long?

Without purchasing one gift, I left the store. Standing in front of Wal-Mart, I shifted the phone to my other ear. Justine kept on talking, oblivious. I heard a text message come through and pulled the phone away from my ear to read it.

"Almost done shopping? I need your input regarding tonight's dinner."

Mama.

I wanted to respond, of course, but Justine kept on going.

Mama's next text, "Call me as soon as you can," gave me the excuse I needed to end the call with Justine. Had something happened to one of the kids?

"Justine, I have to go."

"W-what? But I was right in the middle of—"

"Just got a text from my mom. She needs me to call her. She's watching the kids. Something must've gone wrong."

"Of course. But call me tomorrow morning, okay? I really need to figure this out before I go crazy."

One of us was sure to go crazy, but I wasn't sure it would be Justine. Not the way things were headed. I needed a break. A chance to just be me. . .no weddings, no planning, no stars, no gazebos. I needed. . .a vacation. Truly. I needed a getaway from the madness. But first, I needed to call my mother. These days, it seemed I hardly talked to her. She was always so busy at the opera house and I was. . .well, always so busy. Period. I punched in her number and waited.

"H-hello?" Sniffles from Mama's end of the line clued me in to the fact that something must've gone terribly wrong.

"Mama? What happened? Is it Pop?"

"No, you're father's fine. So far."

"Who, then?" I did my best to keep my voice steady. "Oh, no. Please don't tell me it's Rosie. I know she tried to stick one of your hairpins into an electrical outlet last time I left her there. Tell me she's—"

"She's fine, Bella. All the kids are fine. Sophia's got them watching a movie on TV."

"Then. . .what?' Are you ill?"

"No." Mama paused and the sniffles intensified. "I. . .I'm incapable."

"You're what?"

Her voice grew muffled. "I stink at cooking." She sighed, and, for a moment, I could picture her taking the spatula and flinging it across the room.

"I'm hopeless." She groaned. Loudly. "Rosa and Laz always take care of everything. Your poor father is going to starve to death while they're gone." She paused. "How long can a man go without eating before he withers up and dies? I'm only asking out of curiosity."

"Jesus fasted for forty days and forty nights, Mama."

"Well, yes, but that's hardly a fair comparison. Your father is a mere mortal. Oh, my poor Cosmo. I can see his ribs."

"Hardly. Trust me, he won't starve. I have it on good authority he went to Parma John's for lunch."

"Well, that buys me a few hours, anyway." Mama's words were tinged with relief. "But when he gets home and finds out that I couldn't even piece together a decent lasagna, he's going to flip. And when he sees this kitchen. . ."

"I'll help you clean the kitchen, Mama. I'm headed back now."

"But you're so busy. Did you buy the Christmas presents for the kids?"

I groaned and bit back the words "I'm incapable, too," settling only for, "Well, there will always be another day."

"But that doesn't solve the problem of what I'll make for dinner. Unless. . ." Her words drifted off.

"Unless what, Mama?"

"Well, now that I think of it, I do have one thought in mind. Are you still at Wal-Mart, Bella-Bambina?"

"Yes. I'm outside, but I'm still here."

"Can you run back inside and buy something for me? Please don't judge me, okay?"

"O-okay."

"You'll have to double-bag it and sneak it in the back door. Make sure no one's watching, promise?"

"Sure, I promise. What do you want me to buy, Mama?"

As she whispered the words *frozen lasagna*, I couldn't help but gasp. Boy, oh boy. This wouldn't go over well with the Rossi family. Never in a million, billion years. Still, I did as she asked and then double-bagged the evidence and headed home, ready to see how I could help.

Ten minutes after leaving Wal-Mart I arrived at my childhood home to find things peaceful and still. No doubt Mama was busy cleaning the kitchen. I pulled my car into the driveway and reached for the bag with the frozen lasagna inside, then tiptoed to the back door. When I stepped inside the kitchen I found Mama in a puddle of tears. Wearing no makeup. Crazier still, her teal blouse did not coordinate with the navy slacks. Weird. My always-put-together-Mama had apparently slipped right over the edge.

"Mama?" I couldn't recall the last time I'd seen her in such a frazzled state. Of course, her lip liner was tattooed on, and so was the eyeliner, but with the usual foundation, blush, eyeshadow and lipstick missing, she looked more like Aunt Rosa than herself. Odd.

"Did you get it?" she whispered.

I held up the bag. . .just as Sophia entered the room with her husband Tony at her side.

"Oh, hey Bella. Didn't realize you were back. Just wanted to tell Mama that Tony's here after all, so set an extra place at the table. The kids are watching a movie. Did you get your shopping done?" She glanced at the bag in my hand. "What's in the bag?"

I shoved it behind my back. "Oh, it's a surprise. I'll be right out, okay?"

"For me?" My sister's eyes twinkled. "You shouldn't have, Bella!" She gave me a little wink, then glanced at our mother, her eyes narrowing. No doubt my perfectly-put-together sister couldn't figure out Mama's attire or lack of makeup, either.

Sophia reached inside the fridge for a soda, then headed back to the living room to join the kids, her husband at her side.

Mama glanced my way, her eyes filled with tears. "You can't tell a single, solitary soul. I'll transfer the lasagna to a regular baking dish and no one will know. Promise you won't breathe a word."

Oh, trust me. I won't have to.

They would know after one bite, of course. And there would be plenty of drama to follow. Still, I hated to burst

Mama's bubble, especially with her hopes so high. So, I helped her slide the frozen block of commercial lasagna from the foil pan to a glass one.

"Do we have to thaw it out?" she asked. "Or just put it in the oven?"

I turned the box over and read the instructions. "I guess we just put it in there and let it cook. But it takes two hours, Mama."

"Two hours?" We glanced at the kitchen clock in tandem. Four-thirty.

"Should be just about right." Mama shoved the pan of frozen lasagna—if that's what one wanted to call it—into the oven. "Now, we have to burn the evidence."

"Burn it?"

"Yes. Your father takes out the trash every night. He'll see that box and know what I've done. We have to burn it. I've got a fire going in the fireplace. You put it in there for me?"

"But. . ." I sighed as she pressed the box into my hands. I tore it into pieces and then shoved it into a paper bag I found in the pantry. "Okay, I'll do it."

I carried the bag into the living room where I found the kids and Sophia watching a Disney movie while Tony dozed in Pop's recliner.

"Mama!" Rosie jumped into my arms. The twins squealed from the Pack-and-Play, which caused Tony to stir in the chair.

"Hey, babies. Did you miss me?" I asked.

They giggled and carried on, but I still had to deal with the paper bag and its contents. I carried it over to the fireplace and set it on top of the flames. The bag caught fire and dissolved in an instant, leaving the frozen lasagna box in plain sight.

"What are you doing, Bella?" Sophia gave me an inquisitive look from her spot on the sofa.

"Oh, just stoking the fire." I reached for the poker.

"Stoking the fire?" Her gaze narrowed. "I don't think I've ever heard you use that expression before."

The weirdest chemical smell drifted up from the fireplace. Probably the plastic lining on the lasagna box.

"What *is* that?" Sophia rose and took several quick steps toward the fireplace. I used the poker to shove the box deeper into the flames and the edges curled up as it began to melt.

"Oh, just something Mama gave me." I continued to poke at it. "Maybe they're short on wood for the fireplace?"

"It's a fake log, Bella." My sister pointed down and I pursed my lips as I realized she was right. "You don't usually add stuff to it."

"Well, let's watch the movie, okay?" I turned to face the TV. "Ooh, this is my favorite part." I settled onto the sofa, doing my best to ignore the icky smell from the fireplace.

Well, until Pop showed up a short while later.

"What *is* that?" he asked. "Smells like something from one of the chemical plants in Pasadena."

"Something Bella put in the fireplace," Sophia said and then groaned aloud. "I have no idea but it's giving me a headache."

"Bella?" My father glared at me and then took several steps toward the fireplace. "You put something in there? What was it?"

My heart skipped a beat. "Oh, just a paper bag with a little box inside. It's okay, Pop. It's all burned up now." *Except the plastic film on the box, which is slowly killing us.*

He coughed and waved his hand. "But it's a fake log. We don't—"

"I know, Pop." I did my best not to groan aloud. "Sorry. My bad." I rose and sprinted to the kitchen to check on Mama. "How's it going in here?" I asked.

She peeked inside the oven and shook her head. "Still looks like a frozen blob. Help me, Bella? I bought some bread, but I really don't know what to do with it." Mama pulled out a loaf of French bread and plopped it on the counter.

"Here, let me. I make this for D.J. all the time." I slit the loaf from end to end, added liberal amounts of butter, then added garlic and mozzarella. I wrapped the whole thing in foil and stuck it in the oven alongside the lasagna, which was finally starting to soften up. Maybe Mama could pull this off. I hoped. At least she was giving it a valiant effort.

I joined the kids once again, then returned to the kitchen a short while later to find Mama arguing with Pop about the salad.

"But Rosa never buys her salad in a bag." Pop pointed to the large plastic container of of salad mix Mama was emptying into a bowl.

"I'm not Rosa, Cosmo." My mother's punctuated words carried a hint of anger. "Now, get out of my kitchen while I fix your dinner."

"Is that pasta you're baking?" He reached to open the oven door and she slapped his hand with a dishcloth.

"Get out of my kitchen or you won't eat at all."

"Smells different." He sniffed the air.

"New recipe," she muttered.

A smile lit his face. "Well, good. I can't wait to try it."

As soon as he left the kitchen, Mama's shoulders slumped forward in obvious defeat.

"Chin up, Mama," I said. "You go upstairs and put on some makeup. Change into something fresh. I'll finish the salad."

By the time my brothers arrived, I'd pulled the hot bread from the oven, dressed the salad and kept a watchful eye on the frozen lasagna, which was now bubbling in the glass pan. It didn't look like Rosa's, of course, but smelled pretty good.

Mama arrived in the kitchen a short while later, dressed and perfectly made up.

"Well?" she whispered.

"About to pull it out of the oven now. . ." I reached for a hot pad and grabbed the glass dish from the oven. "See, Mama?"

She clapped her hands together as she saw the bubbling lasagna emerge.

"Ooh! It almost looks like the real deal." She reached into the refrigerator and pulled out a block of mozzarella, which she shredded and laid on top. "That's how she does it, right?"

"Hmm. Looks a little bit like Rosa's." Of course, this was nothing like hers, but I would never say that. No doubt Pop would cover that topic for all of us. And no doubt we would all find out in just a few short minutes.

Chapter Seven

AGAINST THE WIND

"The storm starts, when the drops start dropping,
When the drops stop dropping then the storm starts
stopping." — Dr. Seuss

At six forty-five we gathered around the dining room table, ready for our family feast. I brought the salad and hot bread. Mama followed behind me with the steaming pan of lasagna— an orangy-red mushy mess—which she placed in the center of the large dining table.

"Bon Appetite, Rossi family!" Mama said and then forced a smile.

The whole room grew silent as all of the attendees stared at the lasagna, which started to sink a bit on the edges. Oh boy. This wouldn't end well.

Out of the corner of my eye I caught a glimpse of D.J., who stared with open mouth. I could almost read the words racing through his mind: *What in the world do we have here?* To my right, Holly squirmed in her high chair. Ivy responded by letting out a squeal. I had a feeling it wouldn't be long before everyone in the place was squealing, and not in a good way.

"Imelda?" My father's gaze shifted from the pan to my

mother, then back to the pan. "What is this you've put in front of me?"

"It's. . ." She used the hot pads to fan her face, which had grown red. "It's lasagna, of course. Now, let's pray, folks."

"Looks like we need to," Pop grumbled. "Are you sure this is lasagna?" He leaned forward and sniffed the air. "Maybe you made a mistake?"

"I'm quite sure. I believe I explained that it's a different recipe from Rosa's, but promises to be just as tasty." Mama's jaw flinched. "Now, eat your dinner so that we can watch Brock Benson's new sitcom."

"*That's Life* airs on Mondays. Don't you remember?" He continued to stare at the pan of lasagna. So did everyone else at the table, though no one said a word.

"Mama, this salad looks divine." I forced a smile and reached for the salad tongs. "The olives are beautiful."

"Oh, thank you." Her voice quivered as she reached over to cut the lasagna. It didn't seem to want to cooperate. "I got them at the farmer's market. And the tomatoes are from Rosa's greenhouse, of course."

"Rosa." Pop sighed and handed his empty plate to Mama, who scooped a healthy portion of the lasagna onto it. In the process, the slippery layers of pasta slid apart, revealing orangish colored layers of sauce. "How many weeks until she gets back?"

"Thirteen days, sixteen hours and six minutes." Mama dabbed at her lips with her napkin. "Not that I'm counting, of course." She glared at my father. "Eat your lasagna, Cosmo."

I passed a bowl of salad my father's way, hoping he would start with that. He took a nibble from his salad and smiled. "Very nice." Then, with everyone looking on in silence, my father took his first bite of the mushy pasta.

It took less than three seconds for his expression to shift from delirious to disgusted. He pulled the fork away and let out a cry. "What *is* this?"

"I told you, it's lasagna." Mama continued to dish the slippery orange layers onto the plates of our family members. "And you will eat it without saying a word or there will be no dessert."

She didn't bother to mention that dessert was a frozen cheesecake she'd only started to thaw a few minutes ago.

Pop took another bite of the pasta and pushed it aside, focusing on his salad. That's pretty much what everyone else at the table did, too, once they'd been served. Mama took her seat and swallowed down a bite of the lasagna. If she hated it as much as the others did, you couldn't tell from the expression on her face. The woman could've won an Academy Award for her performance at the dinner table.

"Yummy," she said, and then wiped her lips. "I just knew I'd love this new recipe. I find it so refreshing to try new things, don't you, Bella?"

"Um, yes." I took a little nibble and forced it down. "I hate to get stuck in a rut."

"I like my rut." Pop's gaze narrowed. "Nothing wrong with a rut, as long as it's a good one."

From the foyer Guido started crooning *Amazing Grace*. Ironic. Looked like Mama needed a hefty dose of that grace right about now, but Pop wasn't keen on dishing it out. He was, apparently, keen on dishing up insults, one after another. Mama glared at him, but he wouldn't seem to let up.

"You know what they say. . .you are what you eat." His stomach rumbled. "I'm an empty, tasteless man."

Mama groaned and slapped herself on the forehead. "Cosmo, I cannot disagree about the tasteless part, but don't be ridiculous about the rest. It's not that bad. You're not going to starve. If you don't like my recipe, then get in the kitchen and make yourself a sandwich."

"Me. . .in the kitchen? But I'm a. . ." He raked his fingers through his thinning hair. "A manly man."

"What does that have to do with anything?" Mama asked. "Laz spends most of his day in the kitchen and you never question his manhood."

"I spend all day in the kitchen at Parma John's, Pop," Nick threw in. "Are you questioning my manhood?"

That shut Pop up, at least for a moment. Unfortunately, my brother's oldest son, Deany-Boy, picked up where my father left off. The chubby teen took a second helping of the lasagna. "Tastes just like the stuff they give us on Thursdays at school. I'm used to it."

"See, Cosmo?" Mama pointed to Deany-Boy. "He loves it."

"I didn't say I loved it." Deany-Boy took another bite then spoke with his mouth full. "Just saying it's familiar."

"Don't go by what he says." Nick rolled his eyes and patted his son on the shoulder. "This boy of mine will eat anything."

"True, that." Pop pressed his fork into the dried edge of lasagna and attempted another nibble, his expression souring at once. He spit it into his napkin and looked my way. "You know your way around the kitchen, right, Bella? Perhaps you could help your Mama until Rosa comes back?"

"Bella's up to her eyeballs in the Collins wedding." These words came from D.J., who finished off the rest of his lasagna without muttering a complaint, then reached for a second helping.

"The meteorologist thing?" Pop asked. "I saw that

60

groom-to-be on PBS the other day. I know his astronomy show is for kids, but the whole thing was nuttier than a fruitcake, if you ask me." He paused and sighed, a dreamy expression on his face. "Fruitcake. You know I was never a fan of the nasty stuff until I tasted Rosa's. Now I'm addicted. Do you think she'll be back in time to make it this year?"

"I don't know, Cosmo." Mama pushed her lasagna around her plate with her fork.

"And what about her cookies?" Deany-Boy asked.

"Christmas won't be Christmas without Rosa's anise cookies and biscotti." For a moment it looked as if my father might cry.

Armando looked up from his salad, eyes wide. "No way. Are you saying there won't be any Christmas cookies this year? What about Cannoli cake? And honey balls?"

"And Neapolitans?" Sophia asked. "And Tiramisu cheesecake?"

"And Panna Cotta." Pop threw in. "It just won't be the same without Rosa's Panna Cotta."

"Hello, people." Scarlet folded her arms at her chest and leaned back in her chair. "Have you all forgotten that Rosa's not the only baker in the family? What am I. . .chopped liver?"

"Well, Rosa specializes in *Italian* baked goods, honey." Armando gave Scarlet a knowing look. "That's different."

Scarlet rolled her eyes and took a bite of the garlic bread.

Deany-Boy rubbed his belly, then shoveled in another mouthful of the orange lasagna. "We're all going to starve if she doesn't get back in time."

Marcella gave him a warning look. "Don't talk with your mouth full, boy."

"Promise me you won't buy any of those fake Christmas cookies from Wal-Mart." Pop turned to face Mama. "You know the ones, loaded with artificial ingredients and preservatives. They'll find our stiff bodies, years from now, loaded with things we should never have eaten."

"For Pete's sake, Cosmo. So much drama." Mama took another nibble of her lasagna. She chased down the tiny bite with a large swing from her water glass. "Let it go."

"I can't." He dabbed at his lips with a cloth napkin. "The idea of eating a boxed cookie has caused me to lose my appetite." He put down his fork and leaned back against his chair, growing silent.

You would've thought someone in the family had just died, based on the somber expressions on every face. There were worse things than boxed cookies, for Pete's sake, but at the moment I couldn't think of a thing. So, I said the only thing that made sense: "Is everyone forgetting that Rosa and Laz will be back in time for Christmas?"

A visible sigh of relief went up from the crowd.

"Well, yes, but she's usually baking the whole month of December," Pop countered.

"And making her homemade candy," Armando threw in. "What will we do without her candy?"

Nick gave Armando a sympathetic look. "If I wasn't so worn out from my hours cooking at Parma Johns I'd take up the slack."

"Oh no you won't." Marcella, Nick's wife, placed her hand on his arm. "You're overworked enough already. I'd rather eat at pizza every meal from now till Christmas than see you take on more work. Promise you won't."

"I promise." He gave her a little smile.

I couldn't help but notice D.J. looking my way. No doubt he wanted to give me the same speech about not over-working. Still, what could I do?

My father pushed his chair back. "I need to excuse myself. Bella put something strange in the fireplace. The smell is affecting my appetite."

Mama glared at Pop. "Don't bite the hand that feeds you, Cosmo."

He looked around, as if perplexed. "There's someone feeding me?" His gaze shot down to the lasagna and he groaned. "I'd like to bite the hand of the person who fed me this." He stood and mumbled under his breath as he stood.

One by one, the others rose and pushed back their chairs.

"We can have our cheesecake in the living room," Mama said. "And watch a show on TV. That will be fun."

I doubted it, but didn't say so. Instead, I tagged along on her heels into the kitchen and watched as she dissolved into a haze of tears. I wanted to wrap my arms around her and tell her this storm would pass. It would, of course. . .just as soon as Rosa and Laz returned home, where they belonged.

Chapter Eight

CANDLE IN THE WIND

"If you want to see the sunshine, you have to weather the storm." — Frank Lane

The following morning the Rossis met on the veranda to begin the process of putting up Christmas decorations at Club Wed. Pop had already hung lights on the front of the wedding facility weeks ago, but the time had come to decorate the gazebo area with white lights, as well. The fine folks at Stages Set Design would handle the stars and snowflakes as we got closer to Justine and Harold's wedding, but lighting up the place with twinkling white lights would get the ball rolling.

When the Rossis decorated, it was a family affair. Pop, Armando and D.J. worked on the lights while Mama, Marcella and I hung Christmas decor inside of the chapel and reception area. Sophia played with the children next door at my parents' house, though Tres insisted he help the menfolk out with the lights.

About an hour into our work, one of the neighbor boys, Dakota, showed up, looking for Deany-Boy. He entered the reception area just as my father came in through the back door. The kid arrived carrying a large bowl of stew, which he ate, one large spoonful after another.

"What have you got there, kid?" My father's eyes bugged as he took in the bowl.

Dakota glanced up, a dreamy expression on his face. "Oh, it's beef stew. Our cook made it. She's almost as good as Rosa." He took another bite, then added, "Almost."

"Do you happen to have her number handy?" Pop's gaze narrowed.

Mama slapped Pop with the rag in her hand. "Get to work, Cosmo," she said. "If we don't whip this place into shape before the paparazzi descend on us, we'll have egg on our face."

"Egg?" My father groaned. "Did you *have* to say egg? I really miss Rosa's omelets, loaded with peppers straight from the garden. Spinach. Prosciutto. Oh, I'm never going to last until she gets back home."

"Wait, Paparazzi?" Dakota's eyes widened. "The media's coming? What kind of wedding is this?"

"The kind with a nutty groom," my father said. His eyes took on a dreamy look. "Ah, nuts. I miss Rosa's pecan pie."

"Just keep yourself busy at the lodge, Cosmo," Mama said. "The time will pass more quickly that way."

"They've got me heading up so many events up at the lodge, I don't know that I can handle any more. It's almost more than I can chew." He paused a moment and a dreamy look came over him. "More than I can chew. Interesting choice of words, since I haven't had a decent meal in nearly a week."

Pop left the room, muttering something about how he was going to starve to death. Dakota followed behind him, which left us ladies in the reception hall alone.

Mama stood in silence for a moment.

"You okay over there?" I asked as I wrangled a fistful of lights.

"Oh, I'm perfect." The edges of her lips curled up in a smile. "Ladies, I just had the best idea in the world. I'm going to hire the Burton's cook to make our meals until Rosa and Laz return."

"But she's already busy making meals for their family." Marcella climbed the step stool to fasten a wreath to the wall.

"I'll just ask her to double whatever she's making," Mama said, a gleam in her eye. "Whatever they're eating at the Burton's, we'll eat at the Rossi's. And I will pay her well—very well—for her time and trouble. But ladies, promise me this. . ." Her words intensified. "Don't. Tell. Cosmo."

"Don't tell him where the food is coming from?" Marcella looked down from her perch, clearly confused.

"Really, Mama?" I asked. "Why not just let him know? Won't it be easier that way?"

"I don't expect you to understand, Bella." Mama's eyes flooded with tears and she set her rag on the table. "It's my pride at stake. Your father cannot know. This is my storm to weather, and I must do so in my own way."

She didn't think he would figure it out when he saw that the kitchen was clean?

Then again, my father rarely ventured into the kitchen. He'd said so, himself. Manly men—fellas in their undershirts—rarely spent time in the kitchen, except, perhaps, to refill their coffee cups in the morning.

Yes, Mama was perfectly safe. Still, I couldn't help but think this latest plan of hers wouldn't end well.

It took several hours to finish our work, but by noon—with most in agreement that we should head to Parma Johns for lunch—we had the place looking really good. D.J. offered to put the ladders away and I headed next door to fetch the kids. As I walked across the front lawn of the wedding facility

I paused to gaze up at the skies, which were cloudy and ominous looking. Hmm. A little shiver wriggled its way down my spine as the cold breeze blew by. I pulled my jacket tighter and kept walking. Sophia met me on the veranda, and I could tell from the troubled look on her face that something had gone wrong.

"Are the kids okay?" I asked. "Rosie's not crying about the thunder, is she?"

"They're fine. And no, Rosie's not crying. I'm worried about Guido, actually."

"G-guido?" Mama joined me on the steps of the veranda. "What's wrong with him?"

"He's not singing, for one thing," Sophia said. "And he hasn't called me any names today at all. He's just sitting very, very still on his perch. Hasn't moved one inch all day."

"Very odd." We walked inside and found Guido on his perch in the front hallway, just as Sophia had described: Still. Quiet. Odd.

Mama turned to face the little guy, her brow wrinkling. I couldn't help but wonder why the bird—such a creature of habit—didn't seem himself today.

"He's always been such a little nuisance, and so noisy," Sophia said. "But today he doesn't want anything to do with me. I reached out to pet him and he pulled away. He just wants to be left alone."

"Maybe he's tired of all of the chaos?" I suggested. "He's finally snapped?"

"Or maybe, just maybe, he's missing Rosa and Laz," Mama said. "They baby him so much. Maybe he's just missing the interaction."

"I guess." Sophia's voice was laced with concern. "I sure hope it's something like that and not an illness." She headed into the living room to round up the children.

Mama sighed and stared at the bird. After a moment, she looked my way. "Bella, I have a confession to make."

"What is it?"

"I, well. . ." She lowered her voice. "It's about Guido."

"Oh, Mama. . .don't tell me. You forgot to feed him?"

"No, I fed him." She paced the hallway, her face pale. "It's *what* I fed him that worries me. See, I didn't want that lasagna to go to waste…"

I felt my breath catch in my throat. "Wait. You fed the bird lasagna?"

"Rosa always feeds him people food."

"Well, yes. Nuts. Fruit. Things like that. But. . .lasagna?"

"I looked it up online. Birds can eat small amounts of plain pasta. As bland as that stuff was, I didn't think it would hurt him. You don't think I. . .well, made him sick, do you?"

"I don't know."

"Oh, I hope not. That would be awful, just awful!" Mama shook her head. "Just to be safe, I think I'd better drop him off at the vet's office on my way to Parma John's."

"Let me." D.J.'s voice sounded. I turned to see him standing behind me holding Rosie in his arms. "I heard the whole thing. Let me take him to the vet."

"You don't mind, D.J.?" Mama's eyes flooded over.

"Not a bit." He looked my way. "You okay to get the kids to the restaurant without me?"

"Of course." I wanted to kiss the man for going out of his way to help my mother. Then again, that's always how it was with D.J. Neeley. The guy lived to bless others. He stopped everything he was doing to take a sick bird to the vet. . .and all so that Mama wouldn't suffer. God bless that cowboy of mine.

I loaded the children into our van and pointed it in the

direction of Parma John's, my thoughts in a whirl. Overhead, the skies grew darker, more ominous. Lightning flashed and Rosie let out a wail. This got the twins worked up. They both started crying. I reached to turn on their favorite CD and before long the music had them calmed down.

Still, I couldn't help but fret over the weather. Seemed like we'd been having a lot of storms lately. Hopefully Justine was right and they would pass before the 19th. And hopefully the temperatures would play nice, too.

As I pulled my vehicle onto The Strand and Parma John's came into view, my thoughts shifted. I couldn't help but think about the storm Mama was going through right now. She hadn't caused it, of course, but now that she'd involved the neighbors' cook...

Hmm.

Hopefully that would end well.

I unloaded the kiddos from the van and headed inside the crowded restaurant, Holly on one hip, Ivy on the other, Rosie's little hand clutched in mine. Just as I walked in the door I got a text from D.J.. I put the twins down and they started to toddle off in opposite directions.

At the vet's office. Waiting. Order me a sausage pizza?

I responded with *Of course* then caught up with the twins and swept them into my arms once again.

The sound of a Dean Martin song playing overhead caused me to smile. . .and to miss Uncle Laz. Not that I had time to think about it for long. The luscious aroma of bubbling, melted cheese mixed with garlic and tomato sauce made my stomach rumble. I looked around for the rest of the family but couldn't find them through the crowd of patrons. I finally located Pop already seated at a table, eating. I took several steps in his direction and plopped Ivy in his lap.

69

"Wow, you made it here fast." I gestured for Tres to take the seat to my dad's right and looked on as Rosie scrambled into the chair on his left.

"Called in my order ahead. And you know why I'm here so fast." He lifted a piece of pizza—fully loaded—and took a big bite. "I'll be taking all of my meals here from now until the 18th, thank you very much. I'm counting down the days till Rosa and Laz come home. I've survived one week but still have two to go. Thanks to your brother and a hefty amount of pizza, I've made it this far. If we left it to your mother, you would've buried me after I took my first—and last—bite of that stuff she called lasagna." He visibly shuddered. "I wouldn't give that mess to the dog."

"Or the parrot." My brother Nick appeared next to us, carrying a large pizza. "You heard that story, right? I got it from Sophia, who overheard Mama telling Bella that she poisoned Guido with that stuff she called lasagna."

My father glanced my way, his eyes widening. "Bella, is this true? Your mother poisoned the bird?'

I couldn't help but groan. Mama would be here any second. Hopefully they wouldn't bring it up and further embarrass her. "Well, poisoned is a strong word," I said at last.

"He's not. . .well, you know. . .dead?"

"No. But he's really sick. D.J. just took him to the vet's office for a check-up."

"And all of this from your mother's cooking?" Pop slapped himself on the forehead.

I spoke above the din of the crowd as the teens at the table next to us grew louder. "Technically, she didn't cook that lasagna. She just heated it. So you can't really blame this on her." I shifted Holly's position on my hip and looked on as my father bounced Ivy on his knee. He somehow still managed to eat his large slice of pizza.

My father swallowed and wiped his lips with the back of his free hand. "Yes, but don't you see? This just proves my point about foods like that. They're loaded with preservatives. Artificial ingredients. That's what's wrong with Guido. He's filled with preservatives. Before you know it, that bird'll be six feet under."

"But beautifully preserved," my brother added, passing back by with empty drink glasses in his hands.

I did my best not to roll my eyes as they carried on. "Nah," I finally managed. "I'm sure he'll be doing better in no time. Besides, we need to stop joking about this. It would kill Laz if he came back to discover Guido had flown off into the great beyond."

"True." This seemed to shut my brother up, though Pop continued to carry on about Mama's cooking. Until she arrived. My mother swept in, helped me locate a couple of high chairs, then joined us for some yummy pizza.

"What took you so long, Imelda?" Pop asked. "Did you get lost?"

"No, I, um. . .well, I had some things to take care of." She gave me a knowing look, followed by a little wink. Ah ha. So, she'd already visited the Burtons' cook. Interesting. I couldn't help but wonder how this would turn out.

The conversation shifted to the weather, and—just about the time our food arrived—D.J. showed up, looking none the worse for the wear.

Mama glanced his way, her eyes growing wide.

"Sorry I'm late, everyone." D.J. pulled his chair up to the table. "Had to see a man about a horse."

Mama cleared her throat. "Is the horse. . .I mean, are they going to have to shoot him?"

"Nah." D.J. grabbed a slice of sausage pizza and plopped it onto a nearby plate. "Poor old fella just needs a few meds and a couple of days' rest."

"Thank you Jesus," Mama whispered, and then took a bite of pizza.

This garnered a suspicious look from my father. "Since when do you care anything about horses, Imelda? Is this some new venture?"

She swallowed and dabbed at her lips with her napkin. "Oh you know me, Cosmo. Always caring about God's creatures. That's all. I'm a softie."

"Then why did you try to poison us with that lasagna?" Pop asked.

"Well, that's a fine kettle of fish, Cosmo." She fussed with her napkin, twisting it in her hands. "These accusations really must stop."

"Fish? Did you have to say fish? He paused. "I sure miss Rosa's fish soup. I can almost taste it now. On a cool day like today, it would be perfect."

Mama grunted then rose and scurried off to the kitchen, muttering something about needing extra napkins.

D.J. and Pop struck up a conversation—thankfully, not about horses—and I tended to the children while eating. These past few years had offered me ample opportunity to learn how to eat and feed four children, all at the same time. Not that I really managed to eat much, but I tried.

Before long Mama returned and Armando joined us, too.

"Scarlet wants you to stop by the bakery before you leave, Bella," my brother said as he pulled up a chair. "She's got some new recipes she thinks you'll like, and she had some questions about the cake for the Collins wedding. Do you mind?"

"Not at all."

"Mmm. I might head there, myself," Pop said. "Scarlet is no Rosa, but her cookies and cakes are pretty good."

"Pretty good?" Armando and I spoke in unison.

Pop grunted. "Okay, very good." He took another slice of pizza and shoveled it down under the watchful glare of my mother.

"Cosmo, you're going to make yourself sick," she said.

"*I'm* going to make myself sick?" He quirked a brow. "I'm just filling the well to the top because I know there won't be any dinner tonight. A man's gotta do what a man's gotta do."

"You might just be very surprised to hear that you're having baked teriyaki chicken, roasted asparagus and double dark chocolate cake with caramel sauce." Mama rose, grabbed our empty plates and headed into the kitchen, carrying on about the amazing meal she would serve him in just a few hours.

Pop did not look convinced. His gaze traveled around the table. "Just pray for me, folks. If I keep eating your mother's food I'll be six feet under, right next to the parrot."

"But beautifully preserved!" D.J. added with a wink.

I slapped him on the arm and then turned my attention to the kids, who had taken to squabbling. Maybe Mama would prove a thing or two to Pop, once she served him a hearty home-cooked meal. Or maybe, just maybe, she'd have to weather this storm a little longer. . .say, until Rosa returned home, safe and sound, and ready to cook.

Chapter Nine

Winter Weather

"Everyone talks about the weather, but no one does anything about it." — Mark Twain

When we finished our lunch D.J. and I made our way to Scarlet's bakery next door. Pausing in the doorway, my eyes fluttered closed. The smell of sugar—divine, powdered sugar—hovered in the air around me. I could feel myself putting on several pounds, just breathing the air. Still, who could resist, especially during the holidays?

And talk about a feast for the eyes! I'd never seen so many themed cookies before. And the cakes! Wow. This whole place was an invitation to enjoy Christmas, one treat at a time.

D.J. cradled Holly in his arms and I held Ivy, but Rosie and Tres took off running toward the cases, oohing and aahing over the luscious treats they saw through the glass.

I'd just settled my sights on a plate of snowflake sugar cookies when Scarlet emerged from the kitchen.

"Bella!" She came out from behind the glass and I noticed her *Let Them Eat Cake* apron was covered in powdered sugar and blobs of icing. Scarlet's hair, usually tidy, was a frizzy mess and the red cheeks clued me in to the fact that she must be working really hard back in the kitchen. Still, I'd never seen such a blissful expression on her face before. Scarlet always looked happy while baking.

She gave me a big hug. "Thanks for stopping by. I've missed you! I've been so busy baking I didn't get to help this morning."

"We managed just fine," I said. "But, Scarlet. . .wow! This is all so amazing. You've outdone yourself." I pointed through the case to a row of delicate little cakes, shaped like snowflakes and embellished with shimmering bits of sparkling sugar to look like glistening white snow. I could practically taste them now. "Scarlet, those little personalized snowflake cakes are divine. Is that coconut on top?"

"Yep. And the inside layers are Italian meringue buttercream. Light and fluffy. Ooh, speaking of fluffy, you need to try a piece of divinity. I'm using a new recipe with a little bit of almond in it. I think it's divine."

"Divine. Divinity." I giggled. "Now I have to have a piece, thank you very much."

D.J. and I got the kids settled down at one of the little tables. Scarlet gave us a few pieces of divinity to share and I ate my piece in three big bites, then licked my fingers clean. Each luscious bit melted like a soft cloud in my mouth, leaving behind the yummy flavor of sugar on my tongue. "Man. I see what you mean. That was the best thing I've eaten in months."

"Thank you." Scarlet's cheeks flushed pink. "Here, have another." She shoved another piece my way and I took it willingly.

"Are you ever going to teach me to bake like this?" I asked. "No pressure, but I'd love to know how to do this. Maybe pass it down to my kids one day?"

"Sure. We could do a baking day. I'd love that."

This, of course, got Tres and Rosie very excited. I had a feeling they'd be quite the handful in the kitchen, but maybe we really could start a new tradition.

I licked the sugary goodness off of my fingers. "For now, we'll take a few of the snowflake cakes and some divinity, too. I know that kids will love it. And Justine will think it's amazing, too. You have to make some for her wedding. They look like little clouds."

"Ooh, good idea." Scarlet laughed. "That girl has her head in the clouds. Never saw anyone as intrigued with the heavens."

I started to dive into a conversation with Scarlet about the wedding but incoming customers sent her off in the opposite direction. Probably for the best. I needed to get these kids home for a long nap, and I had my suspicions D.J. wouldn't be terribly happy with me if I went off on a tangent about my work right now. The poor guy looked like he wanted to take a long winter's nap, if one could judge from his slumped shoulders and sagging eyelids.

We headed home and got the kids settled down. D.J. and I ended up falling asleep in front of the TV. So much for watching a movie together. Who could blame us, though?

Sometime after eight that evening I got a text from Mama. Just six cryptic words: Operation *Feed Your Father* a success.

Alrighty then. Looked like she had things under control with her new plan. Hopefully it would keep Pop pacified until Rosa returned. Maybe Mama could get some rest now, too. The poor woman certainly needed it.

I fell into bed that night, completely exhausted. On Sunday morning I awoke with weather on the brain. Strange, too, because one peek out the window convinced me that the storm outside hadn't let up one little bit. Hmm.

In spite of the icky weather, D.J. and I managed to get the kiddos to church. After getting the children settled into their classes I happened upon my father in the hallway, wandering aimlessly and talking to himself. Very odd.

"Pop?" I paused and gave him a curious look. "You okay?"

"Hmm?" He never looked my way, but continued pacing back and forth.

"What's going on? Is Mama okay?"

"Your mother. . ." He looked around, as if expecting her to materialize.

"Has something happened to her?" D.J. asked, concern lacing his words.

"Yes, something has happened." My father stopped pacing and drew close, his voice lowering to a whisper. "Something very, very odd."

"Odd?" D.J. asked. "How so?"

My father looked back and forth then leaned in close. "She's *cooking*."

"Ah." I drew in a breath, unsure of what to say next. I didn't want to give away my mother's dirty little secret, of course.

"This is problematic?" D.J. asked.

"No." Pop shook his head. "Not problematic. Just. . .curious. The woman is cooking like a pro. Every dish she served me last night was straight off of the Food Network. She's gone from novice to Top Chef in less than twenty-four hours. I find that. . ."

"Suspicious?" D.J. asked.

"Yes, very." Pop leaned against the wall, still looking confused. "Not that I'm complaining. I'm not. I'm well fed and happy." He rubbed his belly, which seemed to be a bit larger than the last time I'd seen him. "Very, very happy."

"So. . . .?" I gave him a curious look. "Why does this trouble you so much?"

"I just feel as if she's hiding something from me. Do you think she's taking cooking lessons?"

"From someone other than Rosa?" I asked. "Absolutely not."

"Maybe that frozen lasagna the other night was just a ruse, something to throw me off-track. Maybe that's the point. She's known how to cook all along and just prefers Rosa to do it. Do you think that's it?"

"I doubt she's known how to cook all along," I said. . .and left it at that.

"Maybe she's buying the food from a restaurant," D.J. suggested.

I felt a twinge of guilt as I heard those words. Still, I didn't want to give away Mama's secret. She'd never live it down if Pop found out the truth.

"I searched the house for evidence of that, but could find nothing." My father shook his head. "I hate to admit it, but when I'm wrong, I'm wrong. Maybe we're witnessing a miracle of biblical proportions. Who knows."

From inside the church the sound of music startled us to attention. The service was starting without us. No doubt Mama was already seated in the fifth pew on the right, her usual spot. We tagged along on Pop's heels and inched our way into the designated pew. I couldn't help but notice Mama's upturned lips as she sang the opening hymn in joyous praise.

I thought about her devious plan all the way through the service. Right or wrong, at least she'd come up with a way to stop my father from cutting her down. I had to give it to her for that.

When the service ended, my father rose and rubbed his belly. "Who's up for seafood?" he asked. "Gaidos. My treat."

"Eat light, Cosmo," Mama said. "I've planned a wonderful beef stroganoff for dinner, along with creamed spinach and baby carrots. Oh, and angel food cake for dessert. With strawberries and whipped cream. Light and fluffy, just like you like it. Easy on the hips but luscious on the lips." She gave him a playful wink.

Oh boy.

"Mmm." He slipped his arm over her shoulder. "Well then, I shall eat light at lunch so that I can enjoy my wife's wonderful cooking at dinner."

"Gaidos sounds good to me," D.J. said. "As long as we get the kids home in time to rest."

We joined the family for lunch and then—bone tired and ready for the clouds to lift—headed home. By the time we pulled into the driveway the babies were crying and Tres and Rosie were squabbling. Lovely. Time for another nap. We got them situated in bed and then we settled onto the couch.

I reached for my laptop—nothing unusual there—but D.J. gave me a "What are you doing?" look.

"Sorry, babe. Just have some loose ends to tie up. The wedding's in less than two weeks, you know, and I—"

My husband released an exaggerated sigh and reached for the TV remote. "Bella, I know you're excited about this wedding. And the next one, and the one after that."

"Right. I love my work."

"Clearly." He gave me a pensive look.

I pushed the laptop aside and stood up. "Go ahead. Say it. I can take it, D.J."

"Say that you work too hard? Say you're killing

yourself? Say that, between your family obligations and Club Wed, you're exhausting yourself?"

"No, we've already established all of that. Say that I'm not doing a good job balancing life at home with life at work."

He flinched and I could see his jaw tighten. "I would never say that."

"But you *think* it." I didn't mean to point my index finger at him, but there it was. I pulled it back in a hurry. "Right?"

"Wrong. I don't think that. I'm just worried that you have so much going on inside that head of yours that you don't really relax on days like today—Sunday, a day of rest—to recharge. You know?"

"I rested yesterday."

"You worked all morning and then crashed in the afternoon. Your body was worn out."

"Right, but what am I supposed to do? I run a business, D.J."

"I know. I run one, too."

For a moment, neither of us said anything.

D.J. finally broke the silence. "Anyway, I think you need to take a few hours for yourself. For. . .us."

I took a seat next to him on the sofa and leaned against him, unable to come up with anything rational to say in response. How could I argue with a man who just wanted to spend time with me?

After a few minutes, he placed a little kiss in my hair.

"We need to talk about Christmas plans," I said after a moment of thoughtful reflection.

"Christmas?" He sounded perplexed. "What's to talk about? It's the same every year."

"That's kind of what I wanted to talk about. Your parents have that motorcycle outreach on Christmas Day."

"Right, but they're free on Christmas Eve. Mom called a couple of days ago to see if we might want to come out to Splendora to spend the night."

"But if we spend Christmas Eve night in Splendora—like we did last year and the year before—then the kids won't be here—at our house—to open their gifts on Christmas morning."

"Well, yeah, but we could take their presents with us, like we did last year. Remember? It worked out pretty well."

"I don't know, D.J. Just seems like nothing feels right this year. Everything is out of sorts. I'd like the kids to have some sort of stability. Something normal."

"Normal?" He laughed. "Did you really just use the word normal to describe our lives?" His chuckle put me on edge. "You, the one who can't even put her laptop down for five minutes."

"Well, you know what I mean. Christmas morning is the only time that we have with just us and the kids. Once we hit the noon hour it's Christmas dinner at the Rossi home. I love it, but. . ."

"You're wanting to stay home this Christmas?"

"Just in the morning. Just so the kids can be with us. You. Me. The kids. No one else."

"Okay, so we drive out to Splendora on Christmas Eve and drive back that same night?"

"Would you mind?" I didn't mean to pout, but I did. "We could make it special. Open presents with your parents. Get the kids in their jammies. Have hot chocolate. Then drive home with Christmas music playing. Maybe look at lights on houses as we go?"

I like that idea. Mama will send us on our way with plenty of sweets. She's already told me about the snowball

81

cookies she's making. And the pies. Lots and lots of pies."

"Sounds amazing." I could practically taste it all now.

"So, about your work schedule. . ." He cleared his throat.

I did my best to look convincing as I gave him an impassioned speech. "I promise, as soon as Justine's wedding is behind me, there are no more events until after Christmas." I paused. "Well, I've rented the reception hall out to a small insurance company for a Christmas dinner, but nothing else." Another pause followed as I thought it through. "Ooh, and there's a women's auxiliary luncheon—a Christmas themed auction, really—on the 20th. Mama's hosting that one. Oh, and she's got an opera guild event on the 21st, too, but I'm not really expected to be all that involved. Well, except for setup and breakdown."

I thought Club Wed was a wedding facility." D.J. raked his fingers through that gorgeous hair of his. "When did we become an all-purpose venue?"

"Not sure. Just seemed like a natural progression. People need a gathering place and Club Wed is the best choice."

"For them or for us?" He paused and I could read the worry etched in his brow. "I'm just worried about you, Bella. You're taking on too much. Kids. House. Work. Wedding after wedding. It would be one thing if your work stopped at the office, but you're on the go around the clock. Sometimes I wish. . ." He pursed his lips and shook his head.

"What?"

"Sometimes I wish you had an off switch." He put his hand up. "And I don't mean that like it sounds."

How else could he mean it? The man wished I had an off switch? Did he get tired of listening to me ramble on and on about weddings?

For the first time since we started this conversation I

realized he still had the TV remote in his hand. With the flip of a wrist he hit the button and the screen lit up. Lovely. A football game. D.J. settled back against the sofa, his gaze shifting from me to the game.

Well, great.

I reached for my laptop, ready to get to work.

Chapter Ten

CALM AFTER THE STORM

"Then come the wild weather, come sleet or come snow, we will stand by each other, however it blow." — Simon Dach

By Monday morning the clouds had lifted—both physically and emotionally. I started my work day at home, making phone call after phone call to vendor after vendor, all in preparation for Justine and Harold's big day. Then I dropped the kids off at our church's Mother's Day Out program and headed to Club Wed. I'd almost arrived when my cell phone rang. My car's Bluetooth picked it up and I answered with a hesitant, "Hello?" unsure of who I'd find on the other end of the line.

"Mrs. Neeley, this is Doctor Jamison at *Love Your Pet* Veterinary Specialists. Guido is ready to go home."

"Oh, I see." I pulled the car into the driveway at the wedding facility and turned off the engine. "Did you call his owner?"

"Lazarro Rossi? I believe your husband said he was out of the country?"

"No, I meant my mother, Imelda Rossi. But, never mind. I'll call her, myself. Hopefully she'll be right in to pick him up. I have a full day, so I won't be available, sorry."

I ended the call and telephoned my mother, who didn't answer until the fourth ring.

"Bella, is everything all right?" she asked, her words rushed.

"Yes. I just got a call from the vet's office. Guido's ready to be picked up."

"I'm sorry, honey, but I'm heading out to do some Christmas shopping. Would you like to join me? We could have a girls' day."

"I wish I had time, Mama, but I'm up to my eyeballs in this wedding stuff. Oh, and I need to figure out the whole Guido thing. He's—"

"I understand busy. I surely do. Still playing catch-up, myself. But things are a little better, now that I have our meals under control. It's worked like a charm. I've been ordering our meals every night. The Burtons' cook is simply amazing. Best of all, she's sworn to secrecy, so no one will ever know, even the Burtons."

"But how are you sneaking it in without Pop seeing?"

"Easy. I gave Dakota a key to our house and he brings the food over at five o'clock while your father is still at the lodge or at Parma John's or the gym. Whatever. I get home just in time to warm it up in the oven or microwave, so by the time your father walks in, the whole house smells divine. Tonight we're having pot roast with potatoes and carrots. From what I hear, it's the best in town."

"Sounds amazing. But don't you think this is a little. . .deceptive?"

"Oh, I've never told him that I'm making the meals," she said. "Just don't mention it. He eats and is happy. I clean up afterwards and I'm happy. Then I write a check to the real chef for services rendered. She's happy, I'm happy, we're all happy."

"And Pop won't figure it all out when he sees the checks?"

"I take care of the finances, Bella. He rarely looks at such things. And honestly, the man just wants a good meal. This is the perfect solution."

"Well, I'm glad it's working out for you."

I was glad. And, as I hung up the phone, I realized that I was also glad to see my parents getting along so well.

Then again, I'd be happier if I'd been able to talk Mama into going to fetch Guido. Hmm.

I called my father. Maybe he would run to the vet's office for me. I found him at his lodge meeting, deep in a conversation with the men about donating eyeglasses to a foreign missions organization. So much for that idea.

I called my sister, but she gave me a quick "No."

"Sorry, Bella, but I've got Deany-Boy and Frankie today. We're going to see that new Christmas movie, the one set in France. Speaking of which, did you see that Rosa and Laz sent postcards from Paris? I'm so jealous! I've been dying to go to Paris my whole life. It's not fair that they get to go and I don't, right?" She lit into a tangent about France and I sighed. Looked like I'd be going to fetch the bird after all.

I turned the car back on and headed out to the vet's office. When I arrived, I found Guido looking much perkier than before. He trilled a funny little tune and then cried out "Bella-Bambina!" and I reached to pet him. Alrighty then.

"How's our patient?" I asked the vet.

Dr. Jamison opened the bird's chart and peered inside, then ran his finger down Guido's back. "Physically, I think he's going to do fine. And just for the record, I'm not sure his illness was related to anything he ate, so please tell your mom to rest easy."

"Really?"

"Yeah, I think he had some sort of infection, which we treated with an antibiotic. But I honestly think there's more going on than that. Something that might require long-term care."

"Long term care?" My heart *thump-thumped*. Oh boy. Now what? That's all we needed. . .a chronically ill parrot. How would I break the news to Laz?

The vet thumbed through the chart, his finger finally landing on something he'd scribbled down. "I believe Guido is suffering from a condition called S.A.D.," the vet explained.

I posed the obvious question: "What's S.A.D.?"

The vet reached over to stroke Guido on the back once again. "Separation Anxiety Disorder." He lowered his voice, now speaking in a strained whisper. "Animals know when their owners are gone and they mourn their loss."

"Seriously?"

"Yes. We see this in dogs all the time, especially those whose owners work outside the home. They begin to act up, or—in Guido's case—shut down. Some stop eating. I've seen crazy extremes—dogs that get overly-hyper, eating everything in sight. Cats that vomit. Birds that stop singing." He gave a little shrug. "When are Rosa and Laz coming back?"

"Ten more days," I said. "And just for the record, we're all mourning their loss, so I guess you could say the whole family has S.A.D." I laughed, but it didn't feel so funny.

"I'm sure you're all missing them, but S.A.D. makes animals—and probably people, too—do strange things."

"Like?"

"Like, in Guido's case, pluck his feathers out. Did you

87

notice he's missing a few?"

"Yes, but I thought maybe it was his allergies acting up again." I gave the little guy a closer look. Sure enough, the vet was right. Why hadn't we noticed? Ah yes, we were too busy working ourselves to death.

"My tech observed him in action," Dr. Jamison added. "And the little sores on his belly? They're self-induced."

Whoa. The bird was biting himself?

"So, what do we do?" I asked.

Dr. Jamison closed the chart and focused on Guido, who'd taken to singing. "Anti-anxiety meds. They will calm him right down and will probably ease the stomach discomfort, too. A lot of his tummy issues are actually mental, not physical."

Great. So now our bird had mental problems. Join the family.

"Do you have to give the meds to the bird?" I asked. "Couldn't you just give them to the rest of us?" I offered a strained laugh and the vet chuckled in response.

"Well, I'm not against people taking medication when necessary, but in your case, if you're missing Rosa and Laz to the point where it's affecting the family, you might look at a completely different kind of prescription."

"What's that?"

"Togetherness."

"Huh?"

"Most people—and animals—just need the steady reminder that they're surrounded by people they love. They need reassurance. You can give Guido that with your consistent presence. Talk to him. Love on him. Give him all the time you can."

For whatever reason, my thoughts sailed straight to

D.J.'s attitude, of late. So, that's what was wrong with him lately. I hadn't given him a steady reminder that I was there for him. That I had his back. I'd been so busy rushing here and there, taking care of others, that he felt left out. S.A.D.

I released a slow breath. "Dr. Jamison, you've helped more than you know. I owe you."

"Yes, you do. The tech will bring you the bill in a moment, and it includes Guido's overnight care, meds and the antibiotic he received via IV while visiting us." He listed the various other items on the bill, but I didn't mind. It would be worth it all, just to know that the sadness—er, S.A.D.ness—could be addressed by simply caring more. Spending more time with. Loving on. In short, by doing the things that the Lord had already commanded me to do in his Word. Not just with the bird, but the ones I loved, as well.

I took Guido back to Club Wed with me, determined to keep him occupied until my parents arrived home. No more S.A.D.ness for Guido. Not if I could help it.

Only, I found myself so engrossed in my work that I forgot to talk to him. In fact, I also forgot to pick up the kids from Mother's Day Out. Only when I received a call from D.J. did it hit me.

"Um, Bella?"

"D.J.! What time is it?"

"Three-thirty. You were supposed to get the kids at three. . .at the latest."

"I. . .I. . ." I glanced at the clock, unsure of how so much time had passed. "I'm so sorry."

"They tried to reach you, but you didn't answer."

"I've been on the phone most of the day, sorry. Must've missed the call. But I can leave now."

"No point. I picked up the kids and brought them home.

You just finish whatever you need to do. I'll see you when you're done."

I'd just started to say, "Okay, thanks" when he abruptly ended the call.

Well, great. Maybe D.J. wasn't just S.A.D. Maybe he was also a little M.A.D. But what could I do about that here? I'd better finish my work and head home.

Only, I had a couple more calls to make. By the time I finished the last one—and tidied up the accounting for the upcoming wedding—the clock read 5:30. No. Way. I'd done it again. I shot out of my chair, took Guido from his perch, and headed next door to my parents' place.

As I walked into the foyer, the most delicious aroma greeted me. I settled Guido in his cage then walked into the kitchen to find Mama and my Pop seated at the little breakfast table—just the two of them—enjoying what looked like a feast fit for a king. The smell of the pot roast took my breath away and made my mouth water.

"Ooh, Bella!" Mama sprang to her feet and reached for an empty bowl. "You want to join us? We've got plenty."

"Your mother made enough for an army." My father laughed. "But I'm not complaining. Those Food Network shows she's been watching are finally paying off."

I gave my mother a "What's he talking about?" look and she simply smiled—a broad, fake, "Please keep your mouth shut" smile.

"The point is, we've got plenty." Mama passed a bowl my way. "Would you like to eat?"

"No, I have to get home to fix dinner for D.J. and the kids."

"Well, I have the perfect solution. I'll put a huge portion of the leftovers in a to-go container and you can take it with you. Then you won't have to cook. Sound good?"

Pop started to grumble about how he'd hoped to eat the leftovers tomorrow, but Mama scolded him. "There will be plenty left for you, Cosmo. You don't want your daughter and grandchildren to starve, do you?"

"Well. . ." He sighed. "I guess not."

"Besides, I'll be fixing a yummy meal for you tomorrow night, one I think you're really going to enjoy. Pork tenderloin with red potatoes and salad." Mama gave Pop a kiss on the cheek then put together a container filled to the brim with the luscious foods and sent me on my way. I arrived home and carried the food to the kitchen.

I found D.J. on the floor, cleaning up a mess of some sort. He glanced my way.

"Tres knocked over the flour bin and it went everywhere." My husband sighed.

"Kind of looks like it's been snowing in here."

"Snow would've been easier to clean up, I think." He shrugged and stood. "What smells so great?"

"Mama sent me home with pot roast, potatoes and carrots."

"Wait. . .your mother did the cooking and it smells like that?" He gave me an "I'm not buying it" look.

"Well, it's kind of a long story, but trust me when I say that this meal is delicious. And free. Well, free to us, I mean. She paid a hefty price, I'm sure."

"I'll take your word for it." Off in the distance, Holly and Ivy cried. "I think they're hungry," D.J. said. "Or maybe they're not feeling well. They've both been crying ever since I picked them up from Mother's Day Out. I think maybe they're lonely."

The vet's words came to mind and I sighed. "I'm pretty

sure they're S.A.D."

"Sad? About what?" He looked up from his work.

"Kind of a long story. But I know what's wrong with them, and I plan to remedy it."

"Well, I'm glad you have a plan, because I'm up to my eyeballs in clueless." He reached for the broom and swept up the mess.

I went to fetch my daughters. Snuggling them both in my arms, I planted kisses all over those cherub cheeks. The girls cooed with delight and giggled out the word, "Mama."

"S.A.D. no more, right little ones?" I held them close, then carried them both with me into the kitchen, where I shared the sweetest dinner with my little family we'd had in ages. Maybe it was the pot roast. I wasn't sure. But something had all of us smiling.

And the smiles continued after D.J. and I put the kids to bed. He showered first and then I took my turn. Afterwards I dried off and put on my favorite nightie—a lovely pink number that always raised my hubby's eyebrows. When I emerged from the bathroom, D.J.'s eyes lit up. He let out a little whistle and leaned back against the pillows on the bed.

"Wowza. You look. . .amazing."

"In this old thing?" I did a little twirl to show off the nightie and he quirked a brow.

"Yes, in that old thing."

I got into bed and D.J. pulled me into his arms and kissed me like I hadn't been kissed for. . .wow, for years. And then he kissed me some more. As his lips met mine, I sensed his passion, his hunger. How long had I kept this poor guy waiting for an evening of romance with his wife? He'd been too patient. The kiss deepened and I found myself swooning in his arms.

Off in the distance I heard my phone buzz, the familiar sound for a text coming through. I ignored it. It buzzed again.

"Don't worry," I whispered.

About a minute later, just as D.J.'s lips traveled down my neck toward my shoulder, the phone rang. My precious husband paused, then looked at me intently. "Should you get it?"

"Nah. I'm sure it'll wait. This is more important."

I glanced at the cell phone on the bedside table, saw Justine's number. Hmm. Like it or not, she could wait. I was off the clock. And I would remind her—and every other bride—of my hours just as soon as I got back to the office. Which wouldn't be until tomorrow morning at nine. Until then. . .well, until then, I had other things to occupy my time. Like the fella gazing at me with longing in his eyes.

Yep. I had far more exciting ways to spend the night.

Chapter Eleven

BABY, IT'S COLD OUTSIDE

"News events are like Texas weather. If you don't like it, wait a minute." — Jessica Savitch

By the time Friday rolled around I had all of my proverbial ducks in a row. With the help of the events team I'd hired—Stages Set Design—we would have the most spectacular outdoor wedding Galveston Island had ever seen. And, celestial themed, no less, complete with stars, snowflakes, twinkling lights and even—gasp!—real snow. $2500 worth of real snow. I breathed a huge sigh of relief, half-excited to get this show on the road and half-relieved that I still had a week to tie up loose ends.

On Friday evening the Rossi family gathered together for the most scrumptious meal I'd ever eaten: Chicken Cacciatore, garlic bread, traditional Caesar salad and yummy turtle cheesecake. No one asked where the food came from, thank goodness. Mama just served it up with a smile then offered us cups of coffee in the living room while we watched TV.

Armando and Scarlet headed home—something about Scarlet being too tired from baking. The rest of us passed the time until the ten o'clock news came on. Just what we'd all been waiting for. Tonight Justine would introduce three very special guests to her weather program.

I settled onto the sofa and watched as Twila, Bonnie Sue and Jolene walked onto the Channel Eleven set. Me? I would've been a nervous wreck. The ladies seemed perfectly calm.

Their choice in clothing must've made quite an impression on the male reporter, whose eyes were nearly as big as the large yellow buttons on Twila's glittery raincoat. Or, maybe it was Jolene's polka-dotted umbrella that held his gaze. Or perhaps Bonnie Sue's bizarre-looking rain hat and boots. At any rate, the poor fella couldn't seem to find his words once the ladies joined him.

He cleared his throat and stared into the camera. "And now, a special treat as these lovely ladies from Splendora join our own meteorologist, Justine, to deliver tonight's weather report."

Justine introduced the ladies by name and gushed over Bonnie Sue's rain boots, then turned her attention to the camera. "Instead of just giving you tomorrow's weather report, I thought it might be more fun to let my new friends—the Splendora Sunshiners—tell you what you can expect." She gestured to Twila, who ducked under Jolene's umbrella. "Take it away, ladies."

What happened next would be forever etched in my memory. The ladies had apparently come up with detailed choreography for *Stormy Weather*, which involved the umbrella, the raincoat—which Twila removed to reveal a hot pink blouse and slacks underneath. Things were going pretty well until they reached a particular section of music where Bonnie Sue had to twirl. Jolene let go of her umbrella and it took off flying across the studio, jabbing the male newscaster in the head. He let a couple of expletives fly, then quickly recovered just as the umbrella bounced off of the desk and landed on top of a gal holding cue cards. She, too, recovered quickly. The camera swung wide, revealing dazed and confused workers, but the Splendora Sunshiners never seemed to notice. The song kept going. . .and going.

The cameraman, likely energized by all of this action, zeroed in on the ladies, who seemed oblivious to the chaos they had caused. They just kept singing and adding those crazy moves of theirs.

By the time the ladies hit the final chorus, Justine was singing along, tucked under the umbrella with the trio. I couldn't help but think of her as a good sport. When the song ended the news crew clapped and the male reporter straightened his tie, looked straight at the camera and offered a polished smile, along with the words, "Well, I think that went pretty well, don't you? Plenty of sunshine here in the studio with these three ladies around."

Off in the distance, still on live audio feed, I heard Twila's voice. "Jolene, you hit that poor fellow on the head with your umbrella. I think you gave him a concussion."

"Umbrella? Concussion?" Jolene sounded perplexed. "It wasn't my fault. Bonnie's Sue's dance moves caused it."

"Well, isn't that lovely," Bonnie Sue chimed in. "Is that all you can say, after all the time I spent coming up with that choreography? I think our song and dance number went well. Hopefully the folks at home will agree."

At this point, the station returned to their regular broadcasting. Thank goodness.

I looked around the room at my family members, whose eyes were still riveted to the television. Mama finally broke the silence with a contemplative, "Wow."

"Wow is right," I said. "That was. . .really something."

"*What* was Jolene wearing?" Sophia asked. "I couldn't make heads or tails out of it."

"Heads or tails is right," Pop said. "Some sort of costume, I guess. With those gals, you can never tell." He reached for the TV remote and changed the channel.

"Give them a call, Bella," Mama said. "Just to say hello, I mean, and to let them know we watched the program."

Turned out I didn't have to. Just as I grabbed the phone, it rang in my hand. I saw Justine's number come through on the screen and answered with a lively, "Hey, weather girl!"

She laughed. "Were you watching?"

"Um, yeah. It's forever etched in my memory now. Thanks."

"Hahaha. Glad you liked it." Another chuckle emitted from her end of the line. "I've got the ladies on speaker phone. They wanted to talk to you."

I turned my own phone to speaker mode so that my family could hear the conversation.

"We just wanted to thank you for introducing us to Justine, Bella." Twila's voice sounded from the other end of the line. "We had such a good time tonight."

"Yes, we saw that," I responded.

"Was everyone watching?" Twila raised her volume, likely sensing she was speaking to a wider audience than just me.

"We're all here, Twila," Mama called out. "We were watching. Cute raincoat, by the way."

"Thank you! I bought it at the mall. On sale."

"I tried to tell her that color of yellow washed out her complexion," Bonnie Sue chimed in, "But would she listen to me? At least she took it off before the song ended."

"I thought you looked adorable, Twila," my mom said. "You did the town of Splendora proud."

"They did our station proud, too," Justine added. "My producer just told me that the phone has been ringing off the wall ever since we went live. The Splendora Sunshiners have had fourteen offers to appear at local events—one bar mitzvah, and one man wanted to know if Twila was single."

"Heavens." Twila fanned herself. "I hope you told him that I'm happily married. And I'm extremely busy these days. I'm the mayor of Splendora now, you know."

"I didn't know your schedule, for sure, but definitely stopped him when he got to the part where he wanted your email address and phone number." Justine giggled.

"Well now, if that doesn't take the cake." Twila laughed and I could almost envision the look of embarrassment on her face.

At this point the ladies went off on a tangent, talking to each other about their favorite cake flavors, likely forgetting they were still on speaker phone.

"Speaking of taking the cake. . ." Jolene's voice sounded, off in the distance. "That reminds me, didn't Scarlet send a little celebration cake, Justine? I seem to remember hearing her mention something about that last time we were in Galveston."

"Yes, it's in the break room," Justine responded. "The news crew has probably already sliced it up by now."

"I'm sure they wouldn't mind if we had a teensy-tiny piece," Jolene said. "I won't eat much. I'm trying to watch my girlish figure."

"It's getting easier to see every day, Jolene," Bonnie Sue chimed in. "But I must admit, a slice of Scarlet's cake sounds divine right about now. You'll have to have a big piece to celebrate, Justine."

"I can't have any," Justine responded. "I'm gluten-free."

"Well, not me," Bonnie Sue's voice grew more animated. "I didn't fight my way to the top of the food chain to be a vegetarian."

"She's not a vegetarian, Bonnie Sue," Twila said. "She's gluten-free."

"That the same thing as a vegan?" Bonnie Sue asked.

"Vagan?" Jolene gasped. "I knew a vagan once. Don't even get me started on her. Would you believe that woman argued with me about the existence of God?"

"No, not *pagan*, Jolene," Twila responded, and then groaned. "I said *ve*-gan."

"So, you're a vegan, Justine?" Bonnie Sue asked. "It's okay, honey. Jesus loves you, anyway. And you can remedy that problem right here and now by asking Him to live in your heart. That'll put an end to your pagan days and set you on the right track."

"I. . .I'm not a vegan. I'm gluten-free." This, from Justine, who seemed a bit discombobulated.

"I gave up glue in the second grade after Joey Chambers challenged me to swallow down a whole bottle of the icky stuff," Bonnie Sue added. "Not sure my intestines ever recovered. So, I guess you could say I'm *glue*-ten free, too, honey."

"Not glue, Bonnie Sue," Twila said. "She didn't give up glue. She gave up flour."

"Flour? How will you eat your own wedding cake?" Bonnie Sue sounded horrified by this idea.

"Scarlet's going to make a special little cake just for me," Justine responded. "Gluten-free."

"Well, Jesus loves you, anyway, hon." Bonnie Sue released a sigh and then her voice drifted away.

"Oh my goodness, Bella!" Justine cried out. "Are you still

on the phone? I totally forgot I was talking to you."

"I'm here. We all are. And the Splendora Sisters—er, Sunshiners—have that effect on people, trust me."

"Tell me about it," my dad said, and then laughed.

"I'm so sorry. I just called because they wanted me to. Hope I didn't bother you."

"Nope. The whole thing was downright entertaining."

"You can say that again," Pop muttered, turning his attention back to the TV. "Better than *As the World Turns*."

"Just for the record, Justine, I didn't realize you were gluten-free. I'm glad Scarlet knows and can make a cake just for you."

"Yep. She's known all along. But speaking of cake, I'd better go chase down those Splendora ladies. Thanks again for recommending them, Bella. I have a feeling the people at Channel Eleven news won't forget them anytime soon."

"No doubt," Pop said, and then laughed.

Justine ended the call and I turned to face my family.

"Well, *that* was different." D.J. grinned. "Guess they're really putting Splendora on the map."

"Ooh, putting Splendora on the map. I should've had them say something about the wedding facility in Splendora. Those ladies would be great advertisement for us, don't you think?" On and on I went, talking to them about my plans to use the Splendora Sunshiners to promote our new facility in Splendora.

Well, until D.J. glared at me.

"Could we just, for once, have a fun evening without talking about work?" he asked.

"Well, I. . .I. . ." I sighed. "Sorry."

I was, too. And though my plate was full—figuratively speaking—I'd learned my lesson. God first. Family second.

100

Work third. Everything else? Well, everything else could wait for another day.

Chapter Twelve

DON'T LET THE SUN GO DOWN ON ME

"When all is said and done, the weather and love are the two elements about which one can never be sure." — Alice Hoffman

The strangest dreams invaded my sleep that night. In one of them, I danced atop fluffy pillows of white clouds. In another, the Splendora sisters crooned *Stormy Weather* while all of Justine's wedding guests wept. The final dream really took the cake. In that one, D.J. played a Spanish love song on his guitar while the wedding guests danced. Very, very odd.

D.J. and I spent Saturday getting our house Christmas-ready. Mama and Pop watched the kids on Sunday after church so we could drive into Houston to shop for Christmas presents. Though we didn't get everyone on the list, we made a great start of it, filling the back of the family van with toys, electronics and other goodies for family members. I felt much better about the way things were going as we rolled into the new work week. I awoke Monday morning, the 14th, settled and calm.

Well, until Justine called to ask if she could come for an unexpected get-together to discuss last minute plans. I pressed my other work aside and ushered her into the wedding facility an hour later.

"Thanks for meeting with me again on such short notice," Justine said as I led her inside of Club Wed. "I just felt like we needed one more meeting before the wedding to make sure we're on the same page." She giggled as she shifted her purse to the other shoulder. "And I'll be honest, I wanted to see what the gazebo area looked like with lights up."

"You realize the lights are the *only* thing we've put up, right? The set design folks from Stages won't be here until Friday morning to start setting up the chairs and décor."

"I know." She sighed. "I'm impossible, Bella. Now that I'm off of work for the week I just need to be busy. And my mind is reeling with ideas. You'll need to stop me if I talk your ear off. The ideas just keep on coming."

"Might be a little late to add to the plan," I countered.

"Oh, I know."

She followed on my heels as I led the way through the foyer and past the reception hall, where we paused to talk through the layout of where the cake table and other such things would go.

"So, I know it's none of my business, really," I said. "But did you get things squared away regarding the new step-mother? Assuming they're married now?"

"Yeah, they're married. And yes, I got it squared away. Talked to my dad. She's not coming. I hate to hurt her feelings, but she never plays nice and I just can't risk ruining my big day. My dad seemed okay with it. Don't really care what she thinks, if you want the truth."

"Good for you," I said. "Keeping it safe is best for your welfare and the welfare of your guests, too."

"Harold is happier." She grinned. "He was so afraid of drama at the wedding. I assured him I'd keep all my drama on the stage." A giggle followed. "Guess that's my theater background coming out: keep your drama on the stage. Ha."

"Hey, being theatrical is a good thing, especially in your line of work." I led her across the room and through the back door.

"Yeah, well, kind of funny that I'm marrying such a nerd," she said as we stepped outside.

Ouch. Did you really just call your fiancé a nerd?

As if she could read my mind, Justine laughed and waved her hand in my direction. "I know, I know. You can't believe I just said that out loud. But I'm just voicing what he always says, himself. He's such a geek—a science guy who loves astronomy—and I'm such a theatrical drama queen, my emotions changing like the weather. But we're perfect together. Polar opposites."

"*Polar* opposites." I chuckled. "Funny choice of words, all things considered." I gave a little shiver as we stepped out into the crisp, cool air.

Justine laughed. "Must've been a Freudian slip."

I paused before leading her to the gazebo area. "It's great to marry someone who's your opposite. That's exactly what happened with D.J. and me. We're from two completely different worlds. He's a good old Texas boy, through and through. Handsome cowboy material. Me? I'm from a large, loud, obnoxious Italian family. The Rossis hail from New Jersey, by the way."

"Really? You don't have a Jersey accent."

"Well, I've been here since childhood. But I'd never even worn a pair of cowboy—er, cowgirl—boots until a few years ago. And I'd never had chicken fried steak until I met D.J.'s mama. For that matter, I'd never been in a double-wide until that day, either. Our families are different, our customs are different. Our strategies are different. But our hearts—and our outlooks—are the same. We're truly one flesh."

"One flesh?" She looked at me as if those words made no sense at all.

"Yeah, you know. . . *'the two shall become one.'* One flesh."

"Ah, got it. Harold and I call that *One*-derland." A laugh followed on her end. "Get it? One-derland? We always said that would be our wedding theme: Winter One-derland." She smiled, then just as quickly, the smile faded.

"It's perfect." I spoke tenderly. "Especially in light of what your parents have been through."

"Really?" She turned my way and I noticed tears in her eyes. "Because I've been thinking it's, well, ironic. In fact, I almost changed the whole theme when my dad walked out on my mom. I questioned whether or not marriages worked any more. Whether people stayed together."

"I don't want to give a pat answer to that. Even the best of marriages have their struggles. But people can stay together. . .if both parties are grounded and keep God at the center of the relationship."

She looked my way, her brow wrinkled. "What do you mean?"

"Well, take D.J. and me, for instance. Like I said, we're polar opposites, but we make it work. That would never have happened if we leaned on our own strength. There are times when he probably wants to throttle me. . .and vice-versa. Maybe even recently. But if we give Jesus his rightful place— in our hearts and our marriage—then our chances of survival go way, way up."

"Hmm."

I took a few steps toward the gazebo and realized I'd

forgotten to flip the switch to turn on the lights. "Stay here. I'll be right back." I sprinted toward the reception hall, went straight to the light switch, and pressed the button to turn the gazebo area into a twinkling wonderland.

Wonderland. *One*-derland. Ha.

I raced back outside and found Justine turning in circles, arms outstretched. "Oh, Bella!" she crooned. "It's amazing. Gorgeous! Just what I'd hoped for!"

"Glad you like it. Just wait till you see it fully decorated with the snow piled up all around. It'll be breathtaking." I hoped.

She paused, her gaze landing on the nativity, which Pop had set up in the side yard. She took a few slow steps toward it, and I wished I could read her thoughts. Coming to a stop right in front of it, Justine released a slow sigh. "This is beautiful, too, Bella."

"Thank you. It's been in our family for years."

"Reminds me of one my grandmother used to have. She passed away when I was little, but I'll never forget staring at it, wishing I could get inside and play the role of Mary. The nativity almost seems. . .real."

"It is real," I said.

She gave me a curious look. "You trying to tell me those characters come to life at night and dance around in your yard or something?"

"No." I laughed. "But the story is real, which is probably why seeing the display brings on such strong feelings."

A comfortable silence grew between us as we both stared at the baby Jesus in the manger. After a moment, I worked up the courage to share my heart.

"Justine, you're so interested in the heavens. . .in what comes down from the heavens, I mean. Rain. Snow. Sleet.

Hail."

"Right."

"What you're looking at in that nativity scene is, by far, the most amazing gift ever to come down from heaven to earth. That's why it touches your heart."

She looked my way, her gaze narrowing. "What do you mean?"

"That little baby in the manger—He's more than some fictional Christmas story. It's a true story about how much God loves us. He sent his son to the world as a babe in a manger, and all because He loves us so much."

"So, that stuff you were saying about keeping God in the center. . .?" She shifted her position, gazing at the baby once again.

"First, you give him the center place in your heart, then your marriage. From there, just watch and see what he does."

She shrugged. "I don't really know much about all of that, to be honest. But I wish I had your faith, Bella."

"Nah, you don't need mine," I countered. "Your own will do just fine. And if you've got a little time, how about a cup of coffee. We can talk about how you can start that journey in your own heart before your wedding day. What do you say?"

"I say. . ." She looked at the baby Jesus, then back at me. "I say sure. Might as well add God to the equation. As you said, He's the one who created all of this in the first place." She gestured to the skies, bright and clear.

"And He's the one who created the girl who loves it all so much," I added and then gave her a wink. "Your fascination with his creation is a gift, you know."

"You think?"

"Nope." I shook my head. "I don't think. I know."

A lovely smile tipped up the edges of her lips. "Well, in that case, I'd say we have a lot to talk about." She looped her arm through mine and we headed indoors, gabbing all the way. I ushered up a silent prayer that God would give me the right words to share. What better gift could I offer this lovely bride at Christmastime, after all, than the gift of a loving Savior?

Chapter Thirteen

LOOK OUT, SUNSHINE!

"Why wish upon a star when you can pray to the one who created it?" — Author Unknown

The next few days buzzed by. Anticipation built in the Rossi household as we awaited the Friday late-morning return of Rosa and Laz. Armando drove to the airport to fetch them and we all gathered at Parma Johns at eleven-thirty to welcome them back to the island in style. Pop was so excited, he made a large sign that read, "Please don't leave us again!" Mama didn't care much for the sign, but went about her business as usual.

Nick worked in the kitchen, prepping pizzas and pastas and we all waited for the moment when Rosa and Laz would walk through the door.

Thankfully, we didn't have long to wait. At 11:38 the doors of Parma Johns swung wide and my aunt and uncle stepped through. I honestly thought Pop was going to faint. He rushed them, sign in hand, gushing in Italian.

"Thank God you're home!" My father passed the sign off to my mother, opened his arms and swept Rosa in for a warm hug and several kisses into her hair. "We nearly starved."

"Don't be ridiculous, Cosmo," Mama laid the sign down

109

on a nearby table and stepped into the spot beside him. "You've put on five pounds at least since Rosa left and you know it."

This garnered a curious look from my aunt. "How is this? You've gained weight, Cosmo?"

"I'll admit Imelda's cooking has vastly improved in the last week or so," Pop said, "But that first week. . ." He shivered and then took my aunt by the hand. "Rosa, you wouldn't believe what she did. She tried to serve us *frozen* lasagna. From a store. *Frozen* lasagna."

"Imelda?" Aunt Rosa looked Mama's way. "Is this true?"

"Only partially," Mama took several steps toward her. "It wasn't frozen when I served it. I cooked it."

"She warmed it in the oven," Pop said. "In a baking dish. As if we couldn't tell." This garnered a huge laugh from everyone in attendance. Well, all but Mama. And me.

Rosa quirked a brow.

"But the point is, I did my best." Mama gave Rosa a warm hug. "And we survived."

"It sounds as if your cooking skills have come a long way in the past couple weeks if Cosmo has gained five pounds," Rosa said "Such good news. Maybe we can link arms in the kitchen from now on? Two sisters, creating tasty meals together."

"Hmm. Well, we have a lot to talk about. Come, sit, Rosa, and tell us all about your trip. Don't let Cosmo's exaggeration keep you from taking a load off. I know you're exhausted."

My aunt yawned. "Can't believe we made it in one piece. We had a seven-hour layover in New York. Feel like I haven't slept in days. You know how it is when you're traveling. You get road-weary."

"Sky-weary," Laz said, and then laughed.

"But you're here now, and I'm so glad." I wrapped her in a warm embrace. "We missed you so much."

"Missed you too. It's true, what they say. . .there's no place like home." She gestured out of the window. "If we are home, I mean. It's kind of hard to tell to be honest. What's up with these thick gray skies? And it's really cold out. Has it been this way the whole time?"

"No, the temperatures really took a dip overnight." Even as I spoke the words, I found myself confused. Hadn't Justine said her wedding day would be in the 60s?

"Well, it's colder than I expected." Rosa gave a little shiver.

"Yeah." I glanced toward the window. "Hope it clears by tomorrow. We've got that big wedding. The bride insists we're going to have clear skies and the prettiest starry night ever."

"Hmm." Rosa didn't seem convinced. To be honest, I wasn't, either. Hopefully Justine's predictions would come true and this icky cloud covering would dissipate. Quickly. My thoughts shifted to the events team I'd left at Club Wed. Those folks from Stages Set Design had their work cut out for them, decorating the gazebo area in this icky weather.

"The clouds were so thick, I worried that the pilot wouldn't be able to bring the plane in for a landing." Rosa pulled her coat a bit tighter and eased her way down onto a chair, one arthritic joint at a time.

"I just kept thinking about my sweet Guido." Laz's eyes flooded over. "How is my boy?"

"Oh, he's fine." Mama dismissed any concerns with the wave of a hand.

"We had to take him to the vet while you were away," I

111

said. "But he's going to be okay, I promise."

"The vet?" Laz and Rosa spoke in unison.

"What's wrong with Guido?" Laz asked.

"The vet says he had a case of S.A.D.," I explained. "But don't worry, it's not life-threatening. And seeing you and Aunt Rosa again should be just the thing to cure him."

"S.A.D. How very odd." Rosa shrugged. "Well, I'm glad to hear he's going to be alright. We talked about him a lot on our flight. . .what a blessing he's been."

Sounded like they missed the bird almost as much as the people. Oh well, who could blame them?

"Speaking of the plane, have any of you seen the new-fangled planes?" Laz asked. "The Food Network made sure we were bumped up to first class, coming and going."

Rosa's eyes lit up. "Bella, it's a whole different world up there, especially on the bigger planes."

"Remember what I said before I left?" Laz asked. "About the pods? It's all true."

"Yes, they're the cutest little things," Rosa added. She went on to describe the seating on their plane, gushing about their level of comfort, thanks to The Food Network.

Before long, Nick delivered hot pizzas to the table. We sat for what felt like minutes—but when I glanced down at my watch, it was nearly two o'clock. Ack! I had to get back to the wedding facility. . .and quick.

I hated to bother Rosa, knowing she was so exhausted, but she'd promised to help with the star-shaped pastas and other foods for Justine's wedding and we needed to get that ball rolling. As we stood to leave I took a few steps in her direction. "Rosa, I hate to bother you, but. . ."

"I know, I know, Bella." My aunt put her hand on my arm. "I put together a plan during my seven-hour layover.

Take a look." She pulled a piece of paper out of her purse. On the side she'd mapped out a true-to-Rosa plan for the foods she planned to make.

I swept my aunt into my arms and planted a kiss on her cheek. "You. Are. My. Hero."

"What am I. . .chopped liver?" Pop asked. "Didn't I hang the Christmas lights? Didn't I mow the lawn?"

"It's December, Cosmo," Mama said. "The grass was already low."

"I mowed it anyway." Pop said. "Because that's the kind of fella I am. Thoughtful."

"You're my hero, too, Pop. You all are." In that moment, my heart swelled with family pride. "I couldn't do any of this without you guys. You work so hard to make my dreams at Club Wed come true."

"They are our dreams too, Bella," Mama said. "But you work the hardest of all."

"Too hard." These words came from D.J. "But I know you love what you do, so I'm not complaining. I like to see you happy."

"Happy. . .and fulfilled," I explained, and then yawned. "Okay, tired, but fulfilled."

We headed back to the Rossi home. After I checked on the set design folks next door at Club Wed I headed back to the house. I found the menfolk clustered around the television in the living room watching some sort of documentary and the ladies gathered in the kitchen while the children played outdoors under cloudy skies. As we worked together—Mama gleaning all she could from Rosa, who told us amazing stories as she worked—a ruckus sounded from upstairs.

"The boys are at it again," Mama said. "Sounds like they're fighting."

Laz walked into the kitchen a few moments later. "If I didn't know any better, I'd say the heavenly host had descended upon us with trumpet blasts and peals of thunder."

"Sounds like they brought the full orchestra," Rosa said as another crash sounded.

"That's no heavenly choir," D.J. said as he entered the kitchen. "That's the boys fighting over their electronics."

"Good to see things are getting back to normal around here." Pop sat on one of the barstools and watched as Mama and Rosa worked side-by-side cooking.

"Probably wouldn't hurt you to learn a thing or two about cooking, Cosmo." Laz tossed my father an apron. For a moment, Pop stared at the thing, as if trying to figure out what to do with it.

"It's called an apron. You wear it to keep your clothes from getting dirty while you're cooking," Rosa explained.

"Well, I know that, but I'm a man."

"And your point is?" Rosa placed her hands on her hips. "Your brother wears an apron." She gestured to Uncle Laz.

"Well. . .that's different," Pop countered.

"How so?" Rosa asked. "And what about Nick? Doesn't he do all of the cooking at Parma Johns? Or, most of it, anyway? He wears an apron every day of his life."

"Well, yes," Pop said. "But I'm not cut out for it."

"Fine. Have it your way. But the rest of us are going to bond over a batch of homemade pasta. And after that, I'm starting my gravy for tonight's supper." Rosa went back to work, her skill evident in all she did.

From upstairs another crash sounded, followed by kids' voices raised in disharmony. This was followed by the twins' crying from their Pack-and-Play in the living room. Off in the distance the strains of a familiar Dean Martin song played.

DJ's parents arrived at six and we all sat down for a family dinner at the table filled with some of the yummiest looking food I'd ever seen. Before long, everyone was laughing and smiling once again.

Well, all but me. As I pondered the dreary skies, as I thought about the sudden drop in temperatures, I couldn't help but think that a storm was blowing in. . .and it might just prove to be our undoing.

Chapter Fourteen

WHITE CHRISTMAS

"A lot of people like snow. I find it to be an unnecessary freezing of water." — Carl Reiner

On Friday night, after the wedding rehearsal, I tumbled into bed, completely exhausted. I needed a good night's sleep so that I would be fresh as a daisy in the morning.

I had the strangest dreams all night, complete with the weirdest noises: cracking branches. Howling winds.

I awoke to discover the power had gone out in the night. The block on my bedside table was black. Something else seemed off, too. A glare from the window beckoned. So strange. I rose from the bed, careful not to wake D.J. and tiptoed to the window. As I pulled back the curtain, I couldn't help but gasp.

"W-what?"

The front yard was blanketed in white. Snow.

Okay, so I must still be asleep. I was dreaming all of this. I rubbed my eyes and looked again. Sure enough, white snow. Everywhere. Snow on the roofs. Snow on the mailboxes. Snow. . .everywhere.

"D.J.!"

My hubby sat straight up in the bed and stared at me,

eyes wide. "What happened?"

"D.J., come here."

He bounded my way and I pointed out of the window.

"What in the world?" He wiped at the window to get rid of the condensation, then stared out, his eyes narrowing to slits from the glare. "Is that. . ." He swiped at his eyes and stammered, "That's. . .that's. . .that's. . ."

"Right? I know!"

A sense of wonder flooded over me as I looked out at the glistening white snow. In all of my years on Galveston Island, I couldn't remember a morning like this one. Sure, we'd seen frost a few times, but snow? Real, sparkling white crystals dancing across the skies and collecting on the ground below in solid patches? No way!

The children gathered in our room minutes later, *oohing* and *aahing* as they looked out of the window. Tres dressed himself in his warmest clothes and coat and headed to the backyard, ready to build a snowman. I highly doubted we'd accumulated enough snow for that, but I let him think so, regardless.

"What are you going to do about the wedding?" D.J. asked. "Any ideas?"

"Well, for one thing I'm going to cancel the snow order." A nervous chuckle followed on my end. "After that, I'd better check to see if the power is up at the wedding facility. If not, I don't have a clue what we'll do. We can't very well move the service indoors if it's dark inside. You know? I guess candlelight would be an option, but if there's no power, we'll have no sound, no ability to deejay. . .nothing."

I'd rather not think about all that right now, and yet I had no choice.

"Yep." He slipped his arm around my shoulders and

pulled me close. "Bella, just remember, God's in control of all this. The change in weather hasn't taken Him by surprise. Let Him do what He's going to do and trust that it's going to be even better than what you and Justine had planned. Okay?"

"O-okay." Still, I needed to talk to Justine. . .and quick. I'd just reached for my cell phone when it rang. Her name flashed across my screen.

"B-Bella?" I recognized Justine's trembling voice right away. "Houston..er, Galveston, we have a problem."

We did, indeed.

The blubbering on her end made her words difficult to understand.

I slipped into wedding coordinator gear at once, ready to calm my bride down. "Justine, hold on just a minute. Deep breath, girlie."

A pause on her end was followed by a sniffle.

"You wanted a Winter Wonderland wedding. You're going to get a Winter Wonderland wedding.

"I hadn't counted on the real deal," she said. "And I'm going to look like such a goober. All of my predictions were off. Every single one. No starry night. Temps are definitely not in the 60s. And if there's a full moon, we'll never see it. I'll look like an idiot to all of my guest. If they're willing to brave the storm and drive to Galveston, I mean. Most of them know nothing about driving in snow."

"You're going to look brilliant. You promised your guests snow. We've giving them snow. D.J. just reminded me that none of this has taken God by surprise."

"R-right."

"Maybe it's the other way around," I suggested. "Maybe He wanted to surprise *you* by giving you something above and beyond what you could have asked for."

"By making me look like a fool? I predicted clear skies for this weekend and starry skies with a full moon." She sniffled.

"Well, I might have a solution for that part, too," I said. "Let me make a couple of phone calls, okay?"

"Sure, but I don't see how you're going to fix this, Bella. Our guests were promised an outdoor wedding but they'll freeze if we get married in the gazebo."

"The point of getting married outside was to see the stars, right?" I asked. "And now, with the skies so cloudy, you won't be able to see any stars, anyway."

"R-right." She sighed. "Everything is ruined. No stars. No moon. Nothing celestial at all."

"Do you trust me, Justine?"

"Of course. If anyone can salvage this, you can."

"Okay, then give me a few hours. Tonight, I promise, you will get married under twinkling stars and a luscious full moon. I guarantee it." *If we have power, anyway.*

"Cost isn't an object, Bella. You know that. We'll do whatever it takes."

"That helps. And look on the bright side. We've just saved $2500 by not having to bring in fake snow. There is that."

This got a little laugh out of her. Thank goodness.

I ended the call and got busy putting the new plans in motion. My first order of business: call Mama. We needed a starry night set, and we needed it now. If anyone knew how to get one, she did. Mama might not be much help in the kitchen, but she knew a lot about set design, thanks to her work at the Galveston Grand Opera Society.

She answered on the second ring. "Bella, what are we going to do?"

"We're going to have the best Winter Wonderland wedding anyone's ever seen, at least on Galveston Island. But I need your help. That set you guys used at last month's production of *Amahl and the Night Visitors*..."

"Best set design ever. Our guys outdid themselves. But, what about it?"

"I need the number of the set designer. The guy who did the backdrop with the twinkling stars and the moon and all of that."

"Oh, you mean Bob Hendricks? He just put all of that in storage a few weeks back when the show closed."

"He's about to get it back out again."

A couple of minutes later I had Bob's number and an hour later, he met me in the large chapel at Club Wed.

"You want a night sky where?" he asked.

I pointed to the ceiling. "Up there. This whole room has to be transformed into a starry, starry night. And don't worry. . .I've got the guys from Stages Set Design coming to help. They'll give you the manpower you need. We just want to borrow your set pieces as keep you around to supervise how and where everything goes. How does that sound?"

"Complicated. But I'm willing to give it a shot. What date are you looking at?"

"Um, today."

"W-what?" The poor fellow blanched. "You're serious?"

"You have the set pieces at a local storage facility, right?" I glanced at my watch to check the time. Ten-fifteen. "Mama said you're the best in the business. If anyone could pull it off, you could."

"Well, sure, but. . .today?"

Instead of answering his question directly, I played the "You'll be duly compensated" card. Before long, the guy's eyes were shimmering like neon dollar signs. We talked through the particulars and he buzzed out the door, promising to return with a truck and four strong guys capable of pulling off a miracle.

And that's just what we needed. A miracle.

I called the guys from Stages to let them know our plans had changed. They seemed intrigued by the idea of pulling off an indoor wedding and agreed to arrive no later than noon.

Ironically, the Splendora sisters beat them there. They rushed into the reception hall dressed in sparkling winter attire. I'd seen sequins before, but never on a faux fox stole like the one Bonnie Sue wore.

"Bella, we came the minute we heard." Twila peeled off her yellow raincoat. "And we're ready to get to work. What can we do?"

"Hmm. I'll need one of you to help Rosa with the food. She's exhausted."

Bonnie Sue raised her hand. "I can do that. I'll go over as soon as we're done talking."

"Thanks." I paused to think it through. "The set design guys should be here any second. Can one of you ladies oversee the workers in the reception hall and the other in the chapel?" I asked. "I'll be going back and forth while making phone calls and tying up loose ends."

"I'll take the chapel," Twila said. "It's where I'm most at home."

"Guess that leaves me the reception hall," Jolene added. "Tell us the plan, Bella."

And so I did. I filled them in as quickly as I could.

"I just can't believe the way the day is unfolding," I said, after giving them the run-down. "But, as Aunt Rosa always says, 'It is what it is.' The best laid plans of mice and men, and all that."

Twila rested her hand on my arm. "Bella, truth is, you can plan all you want, but in the end, God's gonna have His way. It's easiest just to let Him, and to trust that it's a better way, in the long run."

"Yeah.' I sighed.

"You can have all your ducks in a row and He might just come along and change things at the last minute."

"Kind of like at the fair," Jolene added. "You know that game where you shoot at the ducks and try to knock them down? It's kind of like that."

"Are you saying that God is going to shoot Bella down?" Bonnie Sue fanned herself. "Heavens. Now *there's* an awkward theology."

"No, I'm not saying that, smarty-pants." Jolene rolled her eyes. "I'm not blaming God for the bad things. Not at all. Just saying He can use them for his glory."

"Well, good," Twila said. "Because it's not like the Almighty goes around raining on our parade just to teach us a lesson."

"Speak for yourself. He's whacked me upside the head a time or two." Jolene said. "But my point is, God will have his way—whether it's the weather. . ." She paused and giggled at what she'd just said. "Or, whether it's a relationship."

Our conversation was interrupted by the arrival of the set design folks. Thank goodness. The Splendora sisters insisted on a prayer meeting in the reception hall with all in attendance. After making the fellas remove their baseball caps, Twila dove into a lengthy prayer that all would go well.

I trusted it would.

By three in the afternoon, Club Web was very nearly transformed. I walked into the reception hall and gasped as I saw the set design folks working on the ceiling above. Glittering stars hung on nylon threads, as did snowflakes in abundance. What took my breath away, though, was the ceiling. Draped in black cloth with white twinkling lights peeking through zillions of little holes, it looked, for all the world, like a real night sky. And that moon! I knew the designers had pulled it off with lights, but. . .really? It looked like a full moon, if I ever saw one. I could hardly wait for Justine to see all of this.

Justine! She should be arriving any moment. I rushed to my office to grab my checklist, made a quick call to Nick to check on the food, a text to Scarlet to ask about cake delivery, and then headed to the bridal changing area, to make sure everything was spic-and-span for our incoming bride.

I found Justine had already arrived, bridesmaids in tow. She looked my way and shrugged. "Tell me it's going to be okay, Bella."

"It's going to be okay, Bella," I said, and then winked. "Want to see something?" I asked. "Something pretty special?

"Of course."

I led her to the reception hall and she gasped when she saw the work the set design folks had done. "Oh, Bella!"

"I know, right?"

She gazed upward, eyes wide, and then began to turn in circles, like a small child, arms outstretched. "It's. . .perfect!"

The bridesmaids all stared at the ceiling, clearly mesmerized.

"I can't get over how real it looks," one of them said.

"Full moon and everything." Justine stopped spinning and her eyes filled with tears. "Oh, Bella, you did it."

"No, honey. This was a team effort. They're going to transform the chapel, too. I think they've already moved the scaffolding in there to start. If you like, I can come and get you when they're done."

"No." Justine looked my way, her eyes filling with tears. "Don't. I want to be surprised." She reached for my hand and gave it a squeeze. "Bella, I had everything planned out in my head. I knew just how things were going to go. I thought the day was spoiled, but you. . .you. . ."

I shook my head. "Like I said, it's a team effort. But Justine, I want you to know, you're worth it. Your day is going to be spectacular and it'll be worth every bit of work. The guests will love it, and I'm thrilled you do, too."

"Oh, I do."

She glanced up at the ceiling one last time before I ushered her out of the room with a few words of instruction. "Sophia's coming in fifteen minutes to do your hair and makeup, and Hannah, the photographer, will be here even sooner than that. So, dry those eyes, girl. We've got work to do."

"Yes sir, Cap'n!" She saluted me and I laughed. . .and then gave her a big hug. We would pull off this wedding— with God's help. And it would truly be a Winter One-derland like no one had ever seen.

Chapter Fifteen

STARDUST

"It is no use to grumble and complain; It's just as cheap and easy to rejoice; When God sorts out the weather and sends rain—Why, rain's my choice."
— James Whitcomb Riley

Around three-thirty that afternoon, Gabi Delgado, the bridesmaids and I hovered around Justine as Sophia fixed her hair. Off in the distance, Hannah snapped photographs right and left.

"Oh, Justine, your dress!" Hannah's eyes misted over. She looked at Gabi, then back at the gown. "And I thought mine was the prettiest one ever. This is fabulous. I've never seen so many crystals."

"Austrian." Justine gave a little twirl. "When I stand under the light they twinkle like stars. That's the idea, anyway." For a moment her eyes clouded over. "Of course, I had a lot of ideas and most of them fell apart once the snow storm blew in."

"No, girl." I placed my hand on her arm. "They didn't fall apart at all, remember? When you see the chapel, you're going to be so happy. I promise."

Her nose wrinkled. "You know what? I'm marrying the best guy in the world. I'm here. He's here. The people we love are here. We're getting' hitched! Years from now, that's all that will matter."

"Oh, I don't know," I argued. "I think your wedding day will be as memorable as you had hoped. Maybe more so, thanks to the snowy day."

After a few more photos I decided I'd better double-check the thermostat. No point in freezing our guests out. I headed into the foyer and nearly bumped into Pop, who paced in circles, a concerned expression on his face.

"Pop?"

He looked up. "Oh, hey Bella."

"Pop, what's wrong?"

My father sighed and took a seat on the front hall bench. "What if, say, you knew something about someone? Something they didn't think you knew. But you really knew. Would you mention it?"

I shrugged, more confused than ever. "I guess it would depend on what it was. Are you talking about something that requires a confrontation?"

"No, not a confrontation. I've only just learned that. . .that. . . I mean, I think I suspect that. . ." He scratched his head. "Anyway, I don't know."

"Pop, what's happened? Did one of the workers damage something?"

"No, nothing like that. I just. . ." His words drifted away and his gaze shifted to the floor. "I just have a suspicion about something."

Ack. My heart felt like it hit the floor. So, he'd figured out Mama's little secret, had he?

"Who told you?" I asked.

My father gazed into my eyes. "Wait. . .are you saying you know, too? And, it's true? My suspicions are true?"

126

I nodded. "Yeah. I was sworn to secrecy. But, who told you?"

"No one. That's the point. I'm just guessing."

"Well, you've guessed right, Pop. But Mama wouldn't want you to know. Or, at least she wouldn't want you to act like you know. You know?"

"Wait. . .are we talking about the same thing?" My father looked at me with greater intensity than before. I'm talking about Scarlet. What are you talking about?"

"Scarlet?" I asked. "What about Scarlet?"

"I just helped her set up the cake, and I could swear she seems a little. . ." He paused. "Um, never mind. Sorry I brought it up. But, what in the world are *you* talking about?"

"Oh, nothing." I cleared my throat and turned away from him. "You know what, Pop? I really need to get back to the bride."

"Bella?" My father's voice grew stern. "Hold it just a minute, please. *What* are you talking about?"

"Pop, I can't betray a confidence. I just can't. If Mama finds out I told you, she'll be devastated."

"Mama?" He paused and his eyes clouded over. Just as quickly the clouds seemed to lift and he doubled over with laughter. "Oh, Bella, are you talking about the food? That amazing Food Network-worthy cuisine?" He let out a rip-roaring laugh. "I know where it came from. The Burtons' cook made every bit of it. Er, every *bite* of it."

This certainly stopped me in my tracks. "How. . .how did you know?"

"Dakota, of course. That kid adores me. Your mama thought she could pull one over on me, but it only took a day or two before I caught Dakota sneaking in the kitchen. He spilled the beans."

I sighed.

"Don't worry, kid. That secret's safe with me."

"Let's go back to the thing you said about Scarlet."

"She's in the reception hall. Great cake, by the way. Go check it out." Pop muttered something under his breath then turned and left.

I walked to the reception hall and took several steps toward the cake table, which was fully decked out with the most gorgeous cake I'd ever seen. I stared at it, awed by Scarlet's handiwork. Five super-tall tiers of cake frosted in white cream cheese icing with shimmering sparkles on every level, trimmed out with fondant snowflakes. What really got to me, though, were the stars.

"Scarlet, you've outdone yourself!" I reached to touch one of the stars and she slapped my hand away.

"Have you washed those hands?" she asked.

I pulled back right away.

"The stars are made of Isomalt," Scarlet said with a smile. "Melted sugar, which I molded to look like stars. I put them on the wires before they solidified. Same with the crystals" She pointed to several gorgeous teardrop shaped crystals. They appeared to be dripping down from the tiers above.

"This is the most beautiful cake I've seen from you, Scarlet," I raved. "Truly."

"You should see the inside." She gave me a little wink. "Italian buttercream frosting between the layers with sugar crystals to give it all a little crunch with each bite."

"Sounds dreamy."

"The cake, itself, is dreamy. I went with my fluffiest white cake mix. It's as light as a feather." She paused and her nose wrinkled. "Of course, in this icky weather I worried it would fall flat. You have no idea how humidity affects cakes and cookies."

"I can imagine."

"I think the little star and snowflake cookies turned out nice." She opened one of the bakery boxes and I gasped when I saw the gorgeous glittery stars.

"Scarlet, the gifts just keep on coming. You're a miracle worker. Justine is going to be thrilled."

"Nah." She slipped on food-safe gloves and began the process of moving the cookies out of the box and onto a clear glass tiered stand. After that she went to work unloading the divinity and snowflake cakes, which she'd trimmed out in sugar crystals. "I just wanted everything to be beautiful for her. And now that I've seen the weather. . ." Her gaze shifted to the window. "Well, that poor girl deserves everything inside of this building to be spectacular. So, anything I can do to help."

"I'm sure she'll be tickled pink."

"Ooh, speaking of pink, thanks for the referral. Your Victorian bride. . .the one who's getting married on Valentine's Day? She just hired me to do a scrolled cake with pink flowers galore. Did you realize she's marrying a politician? It's going to be a really big deal, especially with elections coming up."

"Whoa, I had no idea."

"Yeah. From what I understand, it's going to be exquisite. I've been working on my gum-paste peony skills in preparation."

"Whatever you say." I smiled and then watched as she put the finishing touches on the sweets. She stepped back and gave it all a once-over, then—from out of the blue—looked a bit green around the gills. Hmm. A few deep breaths and Scarlet appeared to recover from whatever had hit her. She went to work, clearing the table of bakery boxes. And though she didn't say a word, I realized what Pop must've been hinting at.

"So, um. . ." I reached to help her.

"What?" Scarlet glanced my way, her arms now loaded.

"Let's cut to the chase." I cleared my throat then forged ahead. "You've been more tired than usual lately."

"True." She nodded.

"And I know you work hard. It's the holidays, so you're under a lot of pressure."

"Also true." She nodded.

"But I suspect there's more going on." I paused and gave her a knowing look. "Am I right?"

"Well, there's always more going on in my life, Bella," she said. "More work, more orders, more recipes."

"More news?" I tried.

The edges of her lips curled up in a lovely smile. "Well, since you brought it up. . ."

"I knew it!" I took hold of her arm. "Tell me everything. I want to know."

She glanced around, as if expecting an interruption, then leaned my way and whispered, "Eight weeks. Baby's due mid-summer."

I felt my eyes widen. "Really? Oh, really?" I clamped a hand over my mouth to block the squeal that wanted to escape. Instead, I threw my arms around her neck and whispered, "I knew it!" in her ear, followed by "Congratulations!"

"You two okay over here?" Mama's voice sounded from behind me. She must've entered the reception hall unawares. I released my hold on Scarlet and turned to face her. "Just celebrating the good news?"

"Good news?" Scarlet's face turned, well, scarlet. "How did you know?"

"Because Sophia just told me. She and Tony bought us all tickets to see the Nutcracker tomorrow night!" Mama paused and gave Scarlet a curious look. "Wait a minute. . ."

"Oh, I see." Scarlet giggled.

Mama placed her hand on Scarlet's arm. "Are you saying you have good news, too?"

"Well, I, um . . ." Scarlet looked my way, as if begging for my help.

"Yes, she's got a big order for Valentine's Day," I said. "Victorian wedding. She's doing gum-paste peonies."

"Mm-hmm." Mama's eyes narrowed. "Right."

"It's true, Mama Rossi," Scarlet said. "I am doing a floral cake for Valentine's Day."

"I don't doubt it." Mama gave her a knowing look. "But I suspect there's more to the story than that. . .and I've suspected it for a while now." She patted Scarlet on the arm and then walked away, giggling to herself.

"We plan to tell everyone on Christmas day," Scarlet whispered. "Until then, mum's the word."

'Mum' was the word all right. I got tickled, just thinking about it.

"Hey, want to see the chapel?" I asked. "I need to do some last-minute checking."

"Sure. Let me put these boxes in the kitchen first."

I followed behind her to the facility's spacious kitchen and then we headed to the chapel, where we found Hannah snapping photographs of the magnificent decorations, completely lifelike in appearance.

"Bella!" Scarlet clamped a hand over her mouth and then pulled it away as she gazed up, up, up at the gorgeous ceiling, decked out with starlight décor. "Wow!"

Twinkling stars hovered above our heads, framed in a deep

blackish-blue. The most amazing Christmas trees framed the corners—not traditional, but more like a winter-in-the-forest bare-branched effect. Covered in white lights, of course.

Off in the distance, Hannah snapped more photos then took several steps in our direction.

"Bella, I feel like I've stepped into a Thomas Kincaid painting." She took another picture of the stars. "This is the most brilliant thing I've ever seen."

"I guess we can thank the Grand Opera Society for putting on last month's performance of *Amahl and the Night Visitors.*"

"We can thank the Lord for giving you the idea to borrow their set, for sure." Hannah took another photo. "Glad you thought of it."

"Must've been a God-inspired idea." I glanced around the room, completely overwhelmed at his goodness. "And I have a feeling He's about to give this bride a night she'll never ever forget."

Chapter Sixteen

IN THE CHAPEL IN THE MOONLIGHT

"Under this window in stormy weather I marry this man and woman together; Let none but Him who rules the thunder Put this man and woman asunder." — Jonathan Swift

At five o'clock, the groom and his party arrived in a fabulous limousine. The driver almost missed our driveway, which was covered in snow. Pop ushered them in with the wave of a hand, then got busy trying to sweep the snow away with a large broom. Poor guy. He finally gave up and came at it with the leaf blower. That helped a little. He headed to the facility's parking lot on the south side of the building and did the same thing over there.

By five-thirty the paparazzi had arrived. Well, not really the paparazzi, but the news crew from the station. They were particularly interested in Twila, Jolene and Bonnie Sue, who looked pretty amazing in their wedding attire.

Wedding attire! I headed over to my parents' place to change into my dress, then gave the kiddos a kiss, thanked Deany-Boy and Frankie for watching them, and sprinted back to the wedding facility, ready for the time of my life. As I booked it across the snow-covered lawn, I couldn't help but marvel at how beautiful the whole area looked, covered in white.

I checked on the musicians when I arrived at the wedding facility, then peeked in on the groom and his party before heading to the kitchen to see how Nick, Rosa, Mama and Pop were coming with the food. I had to laugh when I saw my father wearing an apron. He looked my way and shrugged.

"If you can't beat 'em, Bella-Bambina, you might as well join 'em. At least we're not serving frozen lasagna. There is that."

Mama jabbed him with a spoon and spouted off something in Italian.

I laughed and headed to the foyer to begin the process of greeting the guests. Looked like the Splendora Sisters were already taking care of that for me. They gushed over some of the more famous attendees, including the mayor, who seemed pretty taken with them.

"You go on, Bella," Twila said with the wave of a hand. "We were born for this."

They were born for this, all right. . .just like I was born to coordinate weddings.

I made one quick stop at the sound booth at the back of the chapel, where I found D.J. and Armando making some last minute sound checks. They were so glued to their work they didn't even notice me. For a moment, anyway. D.J. finally looked up and gave a little whistle when he saw me in my dress.

"Wow, Bella."

I twirled, showing off the light gray dress with its sparkly trim. "You like?"

"Um, yeah. I like." He quirked a brow. "Very much."

I giggled and Armando cleared his throat. "You guys need to get a room."

"Later." D.J. gave me a little wink. I spun around and gave him a wave, then left the room, my heart in the clouds.

Heart in the clouds. Ha.

Finally! Time to check on the bride. I went back to her room and found her posing with the bridesmaids for some fun photos. Hannah snapped picture after picture, giving instructions. They kept this up until just before seven. I slipped back into the chapel to see if the guests were seated. Unfortunately, the snow had slowed many of them down, so the foyer was fuller than the chapel. No problem. We'd hold off a few minutes.

I snuck back to my office for just a moment, hoping to find my phone. I'd left it somewhere. Hmm. After locating it on my desk I peeked out of the window. I glanced up at the skies but the heavy clouds made it impossible to see even one star. Or the moon, for that matter. But who needed the moon and the stars when one had a reception hall and chapel decorated so beautifully?

A quick peek in the foyer convinced me that we could move forward with the ceremony. We gathered the wedding party together then stood in the hallway outside of the chapel as the grandmothers, then the mothers, were ushered down the aisle. Every time the doors opened I caught a glimpse of the groom, who looked like a nervous wreck.

My gaze shifted to the bride, who stood on her father's arm. He'd come alone. . .without his new wife. That was probably for the best, all things considered. Justine seemed calm, cool and collected. . .until the music shifted to *The Wedding March*. At that point, she looked as if she might be sick.

Until she saw the chapel.

The moment the room came into her view, she gasped

135

and looked my way. "Oh, Bella!" She probably didn't mean to say the words aloud, but there they were. "It's perfect!"

It was, indeed.

And, as the beautiful bride made her way down the aisle underneath a canopy of stars—okay, twinkling lights—I couldn't help but think she'd been right all along. This celestial themed night would be a night to remember.

The ceremony was breathtaking, from start to finish. By the time Justine and Harold said their "I Do's" I truly felt as if we'd pulled off the wedding of the century. And, gauging from the sighs coming from the congregation, they'd loved every minute.

I stood at the back door, ready to usher the new bride and groom into the foyer. They emerged, all smiles, but didn't seem to notice me standing there. They were too busy kissing.

At this point I shifted gears, heading to the reception hall with guests on my heels. Once there I found tables filled with appetizers and other finger foods. This would occupy them while the wedding party had their pictures taken in the chapel.

I walked down the length of the table, taking in the foods, more grateful than ever for Aunt Rosa.

"See that antipasto?" Pop's voice rang out from behind me. He pointed to the tray filled with the yummy, familiar foods.

"Looks good," I said, then gave him a thumbs-up.

"I made it." He squared his shoulders. "What do you think of them apples?"

"I think. . ." I kissed him on the cheek. "You're amazing."

"Well, thank you, Bella-Bambina." He reached to grab one and shoved it in his mouth. "Hope there are some leftovers when this big to-do is over."

I laughed as he sauntered back off to the kitchen. If this kept up, he and Mama would soon be working side-by-side in our family kitchen with Rosa and Laz.

Several minutes later D.J. and Armando shifted to the soundboard in the reception hall and encouraged the guests to start filling their plates with appetizers. I headed back to the chapel, where I found Hannah with the wedding party, shuffling the players around for photo after photo. She caught a glimpse of me and said, "Almost done," then took a couple more.

I led the wedding party to the entrance of the reception hall, where Armando introduced them to the guests, one-by-one. As the bride and groom entered the room, the crowd cheered. The news team filmed the whole thing, their cameraman nibbling on a cookie while working. I also noticed that the news crew filmed the décor, particularly the starry, starry night ceiling. Not that I blamed them. The whole thing was pretty amazing.

After enjoying a marvelous meal, the bride and groom moved to the cake table. Justine took one look at the amazing five-tiered number and her eyes brimmed with tears. She turned to face Scarlet and let out a squeal. "You did it. You really, really did it. It's everything I could've imagined. . .and more."

"Wait till you taste it." Scarlet gave a little wink. "I think you'll be pleased. Light and fluffy with dreamy filling." She led them through the process of cutting the cake and the news crew zoomed in as she shoved a piece in Harold's face. The crowd roared with delight, and all the more as the groom returned the favor.

After the best man offered a toast, Armando opened the dance floor. All of those celestial songs D.J. and I had picked out were played, one by one, as Scarlet sliced and served the cake to the guests. By the time the line thinned out, Scarlet looked exhausted. She took a seat in a nearby chair.

"You okay?" I asked. "Maybe I should've offered to do that for you."

"Nah, it's what I do. I'll be fine." She stretched and glanced at the now-mangled cake. "Heartbreaking, isn't it? All that work, and the cake is gone in a matter of minutes. I guess that's the point, though."

"Yeah."

I looked on as Twila, Bonnie Sue and Jolene took their places at the front of the room. From the sound booth, Armando kicked on the music and the intro to a familiar song played, though I couldn't place the title right away. Only when the ladies lit into *Blue Skies* did I get it. Then, of course, I got tickled. As they crooned the familiar tune, I thought about the skies above—how they'd betrayed us. How the storm had swept in uninvited and unannounced. That's how storms were, I supposed, but this one hadn't taken us down. If anything, it had added an element of surprise to Justine and Harold's big day. And now, as my friends sang about the skies above, I had to laugh.

"Hey, speaking of *Blue Skies*. . ." Scarlet's voice sounded from beside me. "Did she come?"

"Who?"

"Justine's dad's new wife. Didi-what's-her-name. The one who causes all the problems. Did he bring her to the wedding?"

I shook my head. "Nope. No Didi here. The waters are calm."

"I guess that's a good thing?"

"It's what the bride wanted and a bride should get what

she wants on her wedding day." I paused to reconsider that last statement. "Well, I know that brides don't always get everything they want, and sometimes what they want is irrational. But in this case I think it's for the best that Didi stayed home. Things are calmer between Justine's parents."

"Right." Scarlet nodded and took a nibble of cake.

"I met her mom. Seems like a sweet lady."

"You mean that gal right there?" Scarlet pointed to Justine's mother, who took to the dance floor on the arm of the male news reporter from Channel Eleven. "The one dancing with the handsome news guy?"

Whoa. Never saw that one coming.

"I think they make a nice couple, don't you?" Scarlet asked, and then took another bite of cake.

Indeed. They did look rather nice together. And, judging from the stars in her eyes as he swept her into his arms, this would be the first of many dances yet to come.

I leaned against the wall and watched the couples as they danced. My thoughts sailed back, many years, to the night D.J. and I had taken to the floor for our first dance as husband and wife. What a night that had been.

D.J.

I sought him out through the crowd, my gaze landing on him as he worked in the sound booth with Armando. He happened to glance up as I looked his way and the most appealing smile lit his face. Those gorgeous eyes of his twinkled as he gestured for me to join him. I took a couple of steps in his direction, and he headed toward me.

Yep, my Texas cowboy had something on his mind. I had a feeling this handsome fella was about to ask me to dance. And I wouldn't turn him down for anything in the world.

Chapter Seventeen

IN THE MISTY MOONLIGHT

"Aim for the moon. If you miss, you may hit a star."
— W. Clement Stone

By the time the final guest pulled away from Club Wed, the snow was already melting into puddles. I had a feeling tomorrow would be a messy day. Unless it rained, as Justine predicted just before she and Harold got into their limousine to head out. Maybe she would be right this time around. Not that it really mattered. God controlled the weather and He could do whatever He chose to do. We would all just stand back and look on in awe, as we'd done today.

What an amazing day—not just of weather phenomenon, but togetherness. No S.A.D. disease for us! My family, friends and coworkers had pulled together to make this the most amazing Winter Wonderland ever. And now, as the night drew to a close, my feet begged for mercy. I needed to get off of them, but first we had to take care of the clean up. I walked back into the reception hall and found the men—D.J., Armando, Nick, Tony, Pop and Laz, clearing tables. Mama, Rosa, Sophia and the other ladies were hard at work in the kitchen, scraping plates and stacking them to be washed. When I offered to help, Rosa shooed me away.

I headed to the chapel, where I found the Splendora trio singing *Stormy Weather* in gorgeous three-part harmony as they swept up flower petals. Their song came to a grinding halt as I took a seat on one of the pews.

"Don't stop on my account," I said. "I was enjoying it. Immensely."

And so, they continued until the song ended. I clapped with vigor and they all took a deep bow, Jolene nearly losing the large bow in her hair as she bent forward. She managed to catch it before it fell.

"Well, I'd say it's been an eventful day." Bonnie Sue eased her ample frame into the pew beside me and it gave a creak beneath us.

"Has it ever." I yawned. "Weirdest wedding day ever."

"But one of the most beautiful," Twila added with a smile. "Don't you agree?"

"Definitely. Just such a strange thing—a snowstorm in Galveston? Who could've predicted that?"

"For sure, it wasn't in our control," Twila said. "But remember Bella, we can trust God, even in the storms in life. We can't stop 'em. But here's the secret. When the winds are howlin' and—"

"The hound dog's baying at the moon," Bonnie Sue chimed in, her fake eyelashes fluttering with abandon.

Twila rolled her eyes. "The point is, when things are out of your control, you've got to remember that Jesus is in the boat with you."

"We're in a boat?" Bonnie Sue leaned my way to whisper. "This story has a boat?"

"The one in the Bible does," I reminded her. "Jesus in the boat with the disciples."

"Big storm blew up." Twila used her hands in dramatic

fashion. "Everyone panicked. But Jesus. He was sound asleep down below, cool as a kitten, snoring like he didn't have a care in the world. And he didn't. He knew they would be just fine."

Bonnie Sue's eyes misted over. "I get it, ladies. When my Sal passed, I wanted to stay down in the hull of the boat. I was a wreck. And it didn't feel like the storm would ever stop. I could hear those winds howlin' and the waves were rockin' me around. What a disaster."

"A lot of things happen that are out of our control, but we can trust God." Twila stood and started sweeping again. "And there's no better season to be reminded of that. It's Christmas, you know. The season of hope. Trust." She began to sing a familiar Christmas carol as she worked.

Bonnie Sue slipped her arm over my shoulder. "Draw close to those you love this Christmas, Bella. Make sure you tell 'em that you love them."

"I. . .I will."

"And stick as close to D.J. as you possibly can," she added. "You won't get these moments back." Her eyes welled with tears. "Anyone can weather a storm, as long as they stick close to God and close to the people He's put in their lives."

Bonnie Sue's words stuck with me as I left the chapel in search of my sweetheart. I hadn't really thought about the recent weeks as stormy, per se, but they had been rocky. Filled with ups and downs. Like a boat rocking on the water. And yes, there had been moments when I wanted to stick my head under the covers and wish the hard things away. Just snuggle up with my babies and ignore the rest. Perhaps now I could do just that.

I found D.J. shutting down the soundboard in the reception hall. He took one look at my tired self and sighed. "You gonna make it?"

"I think I'll weather the storm."

"Well, good. It's been a great night, Bella. You did a fantastic job." He gave me a little wink and my heart fluttered. The guy still got to me, even after all these years.

"Thank you." I paused and gazed at my handsome husband as he worked. When he finished, I extended my hand. "Come out to the gazebo with me? There's a special surprise."

"Surprise?" His eyebrows arched. "I get nervous whenever you talk about surprises at Club Wed. You're not coordinating another wedding tonight, are you?"

I chuckled. "No, no. Nothing like that, I promise."

"That's good. I'd like to have you to myself for a while."

"Remember that guy from the planetarium who was going to loan Justine his telescope for her big day so that everyone could star-gaze?"

"Right. I remember."

"He came by yesterday and set it up in the gazebo. Of course, he had no idea we'd be facing a snow storm, but I thought you might like to see it."

I gave him my hand and he led the way outside to the gazebo. The twinkling white lights drew us in. I gave a little shiver and he pulled off his suit jacket and slipped it over my shoulders. "There you go, Bella-Bambina. . .to protect you from the cold."

He'd protected me from the cold, all right. For years, now. And I appreciated it more than I could ever convey.

As we stepped into the gazebo, D.J. gasped. "Wow, you said it was a telescope, but I didn't picture anything this huge."

"Right? It's amazing. And such a shame that Justine and her guests never got to use it. Such dreary skies."

We stood in silence for a couple of delicious moments and D.J. wrapped me in a warm embrace. After a while, he startled.

"Bella, look!" He pointed upward to the east and I gasped as I saw the clouds had cleared in one small spot, revealing a gorgeous full moon.

"Oh, D.J." I stared upward, the golden globe completely captivating me. "It's breathtaking. And look at the stars." I pointed to the right of the moon as a multiplicity of twinkling stars came into view. "Justine was right. It *is* a starry night."

"Too bad she didn't get to see it for herself."

I chuckled. "That girl has stars in her eyes. I'm pretty sure she's seeing it now, as they drive back to Houston. Oh, but think about it, D.J. Those same stars, that same moon. . .they've been there all night long. We just couldn't see them. They were hidden by the clouds."

"Yep. That's how life is." We stood in quiet solitude, gazing upward. My heart swelled with joy as D.J. began to quote one of my favorite verses: "When I consider your heavens, the work of your fingers, the moon and the stars, which you have set in place, what is mankind that you are mindful of them, human beings that you care for them? You have made them a little lower than the angels and crowned them with glory and honor. How majestic is your name in all the earth."

In that moment—that holy, peaceful moment—I felt closer to D.J. than ever before. Something about stargazing with him, especially on a night like tonight, with the promise of Christmas fresh in our hearts, gave me a new perspective. There would be plenty of storms to come. No doubt about it. But they didn't matter one little bit.

I extended my hand and said, "Could I have this dance, kind sir?"

"Dance?" He looked around, as if expecting someone to

cue the music.

"Yep, let's dance in the moonlight, D.J.. Isn't that what all of the old married people do on nights like this?"

He swept me into his arms and leaned close, his breath warm on my cheek. "I'm clueless about what the other old married people do, but I'm always happy to dance with my wife."

We spent the next few minutes in a lovely dance. . .until I felt D.J. trembling from the cold.

"We should get inside," I said. I pulled off the jacket and handed it back to him. He slung it over his arm.

"Mm-hmm." He gave me a tender kiss. "Because I have an early Christmas present for you."

"Oh?" My heart skipped a beat. Only six days till Christmas and I still had so much shopping to do. How had he managed to arrange a gift for me so soon?

"Yep." He shivered again and took hold of my hand and led the way down the path toward the building. "I've been working on it for ages now. Rosa and Laz helped."

"Rosa and Laz? But they were in. . ."

"Italy. I know. On a getaway."

I stopped at the door of the reception hall and he opened it. Only, D.J. didn't step inside. Not yet, anyway. Instead, he gazed intensely into my eyes and said, "Every couple needs a getaway."

"Right." Only, he wasn't talking about Rosa and Laz anymore, was he? "D.J.? What *aren't* you saying?"

He reached inside the coat pocket and came out with a brochure. "Just a little something to look at in the moonlight."

I strained to make it out. "What is this?"

"Want to go inside where you can see for yourself?"

"Sure." I slipped my left hand through the crook in his

arm and we stepped inside together. I found Rosa and Mama talking. Pop and Laz hovered around a platter of leftovers, nibbling.

As we entered the room, Rosa glanced my way, the edges of her lips curling up in a smile. I could tell from the expression on her face as she made eye contact with D.J. that she must be keeping some sort of secret. What were they up to?

I glanced down at the brochure, finally able to read it. "Mediterranean. . .what?"

"A cruise, Bella." D.J. pointed at the luxurious ship featured on the front of the brochure. "It's a fifteen-day Mediterranean cruise."

"A-are you serious?" I almost dropped the brochure as excitement took hold.

"Yep. We leave the day after Christmas and come back on January 10th. We fly from Houston to JFK, then set sail out of Athens, headed to Santorini. He pointed to the brochure. Then one more stop in Greece before we hit the ports in Italy. After Italy, we head to Spain."

"I. . .I. . .I. . ." I had to sit down. D.J. brought me a chair. "How can we manage this, D.J.? The kids? Who will. . .what will. . .when will . .?"

"Don't fret, Bella-Bambina," my father said. "Your mama might not be so good with the cooking but she's great with the kids."

Mama rolled her eyes. "And Sophia will help."

"And me." Rosa's eyes brimmed with tears. "Laz and I will do whatever we can to help, Bella. We want you and D.J. to have the time of your lives on this Mediterranean adventure."

"But I have a wedding on the second Saturday in

January," I argued.

"A small one. Simple. I've looked at your calendar." D.J. gave me a knowing look. "Sophia can handle it with the help of your family. Most of your big weddings are in February."

"True." Still. . .the Mediterranean?

I could hardly believe my ears. Leave it to D.J. to surprise me with the cruise of a lifetime. He'd managed to turn this stormy day into a bright and sunny one.

Yep. I had to conclude, this fella still had it. And once we boarded that cruise ship I'd spend every waking moment letting him know just how grateful I was.

He pulled me close and planted half-a-dozen kisses on my cheek, then his lips met mine for a kiss that made my knees buckle. Oh, for a thousand starry nights just like this! Soon. . .very soon. . .we would dance beneath a moonlight night on the Mediterranean Sea. Until then, this crazy Italian girl and her east Texas cowboy would go right on living the most charmed life any two people could ever imagine.

OTHER BOOKS IN THE SERIES (COMING SOON!)

Love Bella and D.J.? Want more? Check out *Tea for Two* (A Victorian Valentine's Day Ceremony), now available.

Also Look For…
- *Pennies from Heaven* (A Springtime Garden Ceremony): April 15th 2016
- *That Lucky Old Sun* (A Galveston Beach Ceremony): July 15th 2016
- *The Tender Trap* (An Autumn Shabby Chic Ceremony): October 15th 2016

Have you read the books that started it all? Bella's story begins here!

THE CLUB WED SERIES
Fools Rush In
Swinging on a Star
It Had to be You

THE BACKSTAGE PASS SERIES
Stars Collide
Hello Hollywood
The Director's Cut

THE WEDDINGS BY DESIGN SERIES
Picture Perfect
The Icing on the Cake
The Dream Dress

A Bouquet of Love

ABOUT THE AUTHOR

Award-winning author Janice Thompson got her start in the industry writing screenplays and musical comedies for the stage. Janice has published over 100 books for the Christian market, crossing genre lines to write cozy mysteries, historicals, romances, nonfiction books, devotionals, children's books and more. She particularly enjoys writing light-hearted, comedic tales because she enjoys making readers laugh. Janice is passionate about her faith and does all she can to share the joy of the Lord with others, which is why she particularly enjoys writing. Her tagline, "Love, Laughter, and Happily Ever Afters!" sums up her take on life.

Janice lives in Spring, Texas, where she leads a rich life with her family, a host of writing friends, and two mischievous dachshunds. When she's not busy writing or playing with her eight grandchildren, she can be found in the kitchen, baking specialty cakes and cookies for friends and loved ones. No matter what Janice is cooking up—books, cakes, cookies or mischief—she does her best to keep the Lord at the center of it all. You can find out more about this wacky author at www.janiceathompson.com.

ACKNOWLEDGMENTS

I'm so grateful to the following:

My Dream Team: What an amazing group of readers and friends you are! I could never publish a book without you! (Truly!) Thanks for proofing my story and for helping with cover ideas. You gals are the best!

My Cover Designer, Shar (from landofawes): Wow, girl! You have worked so hard on my behalf and I'm grateful, grateful. You truly captured the "Once Upon a Moonlight Night" essence in the lovely cover design and I'm tickled pink.

Revell Publishing: Though you didn't publish this particular book, you helped lay the groundwork by publishing those first three Bella books. The rest, as they say, is history!

The MacGregor Literary Agency: Thank you for your undying support, no matter which publishing route I choose.

My Private Indie Facebook Group: You guys are the wheels on my bus, and we all know a bus doesn't get very far without its wheels.

To the Chief Author of my life, the One I turn to, no matter the weather. . .I praise You. You are worthy, in good seasons and bad.

Made in the USA
San Bernardino, CA
15 March 2020